Please
on or be
the last

City College

he has published poems, essays, novels, and translations. He has also edited the story collection *True Tales of American Life*. He lives in Brooklyn, New York.

PAUL AUSTER

In the Country of Last Things

faber and faber

First published in 1987 by Viking Penguin Inc., New York
Published simultaneously in Canada
First published in Great Britain in 1988
by Faber and Faber Limited
3 Queen Square London WC1N 3AU
This paperback edition first published in 1989
This paperback published in 2005

Printed in England by Mackays of Chatham PLC
All rights reserved

Portions of this book first appeared in *The Paris Review*

A CIP record for this book is available from the British Library

ISBN 0-571-22730-9

2 4 6 8 10 9 7 5 3 1

For Siri Hustvedt

Not a great while ago, passing through the gate of dreams, I visited that region of the earth in which lies the famous City of Destruction.

Nathaniel Hawthorne

These are the last things, she wrote. One by one they disappear and never come back. I can tell you of the ones I have seen, of the ones that are no more, but I doubt there will be time. It is all happening too fast now, and I cannot keep up.

I don't expect you to understand. You have seen none of this, and even if you tried, you could not imagine it. These are the last things. A house is there one day, and the next day it is gone. A street you walked down yesterday is no longer there today. Even the weather is in constant flux. A day of sun followed by a day of rain, a day of snow followed by a day of fog, warm then cool, wind then stillness, a stretch of bitter cold, and then today, in the middle of winter, an afternoon of fragrant light, warm to the point of merely sweaters. When you live in the city, you learn to

1

take nothing for granted. Close your eyes for a moment, turn around to look at something else, and the thing that was before you is suddenly gone. Nothing lasts, you see, not even the thoughts inside you. And you mustn't waste your time looking for them. Once a thing is gone, that is the end of it.

This is how I live, her letter continued. I don't eat much. Just enough to keep me going from step to step, and no more. At times my weakness is so great, I feel the next step will never come. But I manage. In spite of the lapses, I keep myself going. You should see how well I manage.

The streets of the city are everywhere, and no two streets are the same. I put one foot in front of the other, and then the other foot in front of the first, and then hope I can do it again. Nothing more than that. You must understand how it is with me now. I move. I breathe what air is given me. I eat as little as I can. No matter what anyone says, the only thing that counts is staying on your feet.

You remember what you said to me before I left. William has disappeared, you said, and no matter how hard I looked, I would never find him. Those were your words. And then I told you that I didn't care what you said, that I was going to find my brother. And then I got on that terrible boat and left you. How long ago was that? I can't remember anymore. Years and years, I think. But that is only a guess. I make no bones about it. I've lost track, and nothing will ever set it right for me.

This much is certain. If not for my hunger, I wouldn't be able to go on. You must get used to doing with as little as you can. By wanting less, you are content with less, and the less you need, the better off you are. That is what the city does to you. It turns your thoughts inside out. It makes

2

you want to live, and at the same time it tries to take your life away from you. There is no escape from this. Either you do or you don't. And if you do, you can't be sure of doing it the next time. And if you don't, you never will again.

I am not sure why I am writing to you now. To be honest, I have barely thought of you since I got here. But suddenly, after all this time, I feel there is something to say, and if I don't quickly write it down, my head will burst. It doesn't matter if you read it. It doesn't even matter if I send it— assuming that could be done. Perhaps it comes down to this. I am writing to you because you know nothing. Because you are far away from me and know nothing.

There are people so thin, she wrote, they are sometimes blown away. The winds in the city are ferocious, always gusting off the river and singing in your ears, always buffeting you back and forth, always swirling papers and garbage in your path. It's not uncommon to see the thinnest people moving about in twos and threes, sometimes whole families, bound together by ropes and chains, to ballast one another against the blasts. Others give up trying to go out altogether, hugging to the doorways and alcoves, until even the fairest sky seems a threat. Better to wait quietly in their corner, they think, than to be dashed against the stones. It is also possible to become so good at not eating that eventually you can eat nothing at all.

It is even worse for the ones who fight their hunger. Thinking about food too much can only lead to trouble. These are the ones who are obsessed, who refuse to give in to the facts. They prowl the streets at all hours, scavenging

3

for morsels, taking enormous risks for even the smallest crumb. No matter how much they are able to find, it will never be enough. They eat without ever filling themselves, tearing into their food with animal haste, their bony fingers picking, their quivering jaws never shut. Most of it dribbles down their chins, and what they manage to swallow, they usually throw up again in a few minutes. It is a slow death, as if food were a fire, a madness, burning them up from within. They think they are eating to stay alive, but in the end they are the ones who are eaten.

As it turns out, food is a complicated business, and unless you learn to accept what is given to you, you will never be at peace with yourself. Shortages are frequent, and a food that has given you pleasure one day will more than likely be gone the next. The municipal markets are probably the safest, most reliable places to shop, but the prices are high and the selections paltry. One day there will be nothing but radishes, another day nothing but stale chocolate cake. To change your diet so often and so drastically can be very hard on the stomach. But the municipal markets have the advantage of being guarded by the police, and at least you know that what you buy there will wind up in your own stomach and not someone else's. Food theft is so common in the streets that it is not even considered a crime any-more. On top of that, the municipal markets are the only legally sanctioned form of food distribution. There are many private food sellers around the city, but their goods can be confiscated at any time. Even those who can afford to pay the police bribes necessary to stay in business still face the constant threat of attacks from thieves. Thieves also plague the customers of the private markets, and it has been sta-tistically proven that one out of every two purchases leads to a robbery. It hardly seems worth it, I think, to risk so much for the fleeting joy of an orange or the taste of boiled ham. But the people are insatiable: hunger is a curse that comes every day, and the stomach is a bottomless pit, a hole as big as the world. The private markets, therefore, do a good business, in spite of the obstacles, picking up from one place and going to another, constantly on the move, appearing for an hour or two somewhere and then vanishing out of sight. One word of warning, however. If you must have the foods from the private markets, then be sure to avoid the renegade grocers, for fraud is rampant, and there are many people who will sell anything just to turn a profit: eggs and oranges filled with sawdust, bottles of piss pretending to be beer. No, there is nothing people will not do, and the sooner you learn that, the better off you will be.

When you walk through the streets, she went on, you must remember to take only one step at a time. Otherwise, falling is inevitable. Your eyes must be constantly open, looking up, looking down, looking ahead, looking behind, on the watch for other bodies, on your guard against the unforeseeable. To collide with someone can be fatal. Two people collide and then start pounding each other with their fists. Or else, they fall to the ground and do not try to get up. Sooner or later, a moment comes when you do not try to get up anymore. Bodies ache, you see, there's no cure for that. And more terribly here than elsewhere.

The rubble is a special problem. You must learn how to manage the unseen furrows, the sudden clusters of rocks, the shallow ruts, so that you do not stumble or hurt your-

5

self. And then there are the tolls, these worst of all, and you must use cunning to avoid them. Wherever buildings have fallen or garbage has gathered, large mounds stand in the middle of the street, blocking all passage. Men build these barricades whenever the materials are at hand, and then they mount them, with clubs, or rifles, or bricks, and wait on their perches for people to pass by. They are in control of the street. If you want to get through, you must give the guards whatever they demand. Sometimes it is money; sometimes it is food; sometimes it is sex. Beatings are commonplace, and every now and then you hear of a murder.

New tolls go up, the old tolls disappear. You can never know which streets to take and which to avoid. Bit by bit, the city robs you of certainty. There can never be any fixed path, and you can survive only if nothing is necessary to you. Without warning, you must be able to change, to drop what you are doing, to reverse. In the end, there is nothing that is not the case. As a consequence, you must learn how to read the signs. When the eyes falter, the nose will sometimes serve. My sense of smell has become unnaturally keen. In spite of the side effects—the sudden nausea, the dizziness, the fear that comes with the rank air invading my body—it protects me when turning corners, and these can be the most dangerous of all. For the tolls have a particular stench that you learn to recognize, even from a great distance. Compounded of stones, of cement, and of wood, the mounds also hold garbage and chips of plaster, and the sun works on this garbage, producing a reek more intense than elsewhere, and the rain works on the plaster, blistering it and melting it, so that it too exudes its own smell, and when the one works on the other, interacting in the

6

alternate fits of dry and damp, the odor of the toll begins to blossom. The essential thing is not to become inured. For habits are deadly. Even if it is for the hundredth time, you must encounter each thing as if you have never known it before. No matter how many times, it must always be the first time. This is next to impossible, I realize, but it is an absolute rule.

You would think that sooner or later it would all come to an end. Things fall apart and vanish, and nothing new is made. People die, and babies refuse to be born. In all the years I have been here, I can't remember seeing a single newborn child. And yet, there are always new people to replace the ones who have vanished. They pour in from the country and the outlying towns, dragging carts piled high with their belongings, sputtering in with broken-down cars, all of them hungry, all of them homeless. Until they have learned the ways of the city, these newcomers are easy victims. Many of them are duped out of their money before the end of the first day. Some people pay for apartments that don't exist, others are lured into giving commissions for jobs that never materialize, still others lay out their savings to buy food that turns out to be painted cardboard. These are only the most ordinary kinds of tricks. I know a man who makes his living by standing in front of the old city hall and asking for money every time one of the new-comers glances at the tower clock. If there is a dispute, his assistant, who poses as a greenhorn, pretends to go through the ritual of looking at the clock and paying him, so that the stranger will think this is the common practice. The startling thing is not that confidence men exist, but that it is so easy for them to get people to part with their money.

For those who have a place to live, there is always the danger they will lose it. Most buildings are not owned by anyone, and therefore you have no rights as a tenant: no lease, no legal leg to stand on if something goes against you. It's not uncommon for people to be forcibly evicted from their apartments and thrown out onto the street. A group barges in on you with rifles and clubs and tells you to get out, and unless you think you can overcome them, what choice do you have? This practice is known as housebreaking, and there are few people in the city who have not lost their homes in this way at one time or another. But even if you are fortunate enough to escape this particular form of eviction, you never know when you will fall prey to one of the phantom landlords. These are extortionists who terrorize nearly every neighborhood in the city, forcing people to pay protection money just to be able to stay in their apartments. They proclaim themselves owners of the building, bilk the occupants, and are almost never opposed.

For those who do not have a home, however, the situation is beyond reprieve. There is no such thing as a vacancy. But still, the rental agencies carry on a sort of business. Every day they place notices in the newspaper, advertising fraudulent apartments in order to attract people to their offices and collect a fee from them. No one is fooled by this practice, yet there are many people willing to sink their last penny into these empty promises. They arrive outside the offices early in the morning and patiently wait in line, sometimes for hours, just to be able to sit with an agent for ten minutes and look at photographs of buildings on tree-lined streets, of comfortable rooms, of apartments furnished with carpets and soft leather chairs—peaceful scenes to evoke the smell of coffee wafting in from the kitchen, the steam of a hot bath, the bright colors of potted plants snug on the sill. It doesn't seem to matter to anyone that these pictures were taken more than ten years ago.

So many of us have become like children again. It's not that we make an effort, you understand, or that anyone is really conscious of it. But when hope disappears, when you find that you have given up hoping even for the possibility of hope, you tend to fill the empty spaces with dreams, little childlike thoughts and stories to keep yourself going. Even the most hardened people have trouble stopping themselves. Without fuss or prelude they break off from what they are doing, sit down, and talk about the desires that have been welling up inside them. Food, of course, is one of the favorite subjects. Often you will overhear a group of people describing a meal in meticulous detail, beginning with the soups and appetizers and slowly working their way to dessert, dwelling on each savor and spice, on all the various aromas and flavors, concentrating now on the method of preparation, now on the effect of the food itself, from the first twinge of taste on the tongue to the gradually expanding sense of peace as the food travels down the throat and arrives in the belly. These conversations sometimes go on for hours, and they have a highly rigorous protocol. You must never laugh, for example, and you must never allow your hunger to get the better of you. No outbursts, no unpremeditated sighs. That would lead to tears, and nothing spoils a food conversation more quickly than tears. For best results, you must allow your mind to leap into the words coming from the mouths of the others. If the words can consume you, you will be able to forget your present

9

hunger and enter what people call the "arena of the sustaining nimbus." There are even those who say there is nutritional value in these food talks—given the proper concentration and an equal desire to believe in the words among those taking part.

All this belongs to the language of ghosts. There are many other possible kinds of talks in this language. Most of them begin when one person says to another: I wish. What they wish for might be anything at all, as long as it is something that cannot happen. I wish the sun would never set. I wish money would grow in my pockets. I wish the city would be like it was in the old days. You get the idea. Absurd and infantile things, with no meaning and no reality. In general, people hold to the belief that however bad things were yesterday, they were better than things are today. What they were like two days ago was even better than yesterday. The farther you go back, the more beautiful and desirable the world becomes. You drag yourself from sleep each morning to face something that is always worse than what you faced the day before, but by talking of the world that existed before you went to sleep, you can delude yourself into thinking that the present day is simply an apparition, no more or less real than the memories of all the other days you carry around inside you.

I understand why people play this game, but I myself have no taste for it. I refuse to speak the language of ghosts, and whenever I hear others speaking it, I walk away or put my hands over my ears. Yes, things have changed for me. You remember what a playful little girl I was. You could never get enough of my stories, of the worlds I used to make up for us to play inside of. The Castle of No Return, the Land of Sadness, the Forest of Forgotten Words. Do you remember them? How I loved to tell you lies, to trick you into believing my stories, and to watch your face turn serious as I led you from one outlandish scene to the next. Then I would tell you it was all made up, and you would start to cry. I think I loved those tears of yours as much as your smile. Yes, I was probably a bit wicked, even in those days, wearing the little frocks my mother used to dress me in, with my skinned and scabby knees, and my little baby's cunt with no hair. But you loved me, didn't you? You loved me until you were insane with it.

Now I am all common sense and hard calculation. I don't want to be like the others. I see what their imaginings do to them, and I will not let that happen to me. The ghost people always die in their sleep. For a month or two they walk around with a strange smile on their face, and a weird glow of otherness hovers around them, as if they have already begun to disappear. The signs are unmistakable, even the forewarning hints: the slight flush to the cheeks, the eyes suddenly a bit bigger than usual, the stuporous shuffle, the foul smell from the lower body. It is probably a happy death, however. I am willing to grant them that. At times I have almost envied them. But finally, I cannot let myself go. I will not allow it. I am going to hold on for as long as I can, even if it kills me.

Other deaths are more dramatic. There are the Runners, for example, a sect of people who run through the streets as fast as they can, flailing their arms wildly about them, punching the air, screaming at the top of their lungs. Most of the time they travel in groups: six, ten, even twenty of them charging down the street together, never stopping for

11

anything in their path, running and running until they drop from exhaustion. The point is to die as quickly as possible, to drive yourself so hard that your heart cannot stand it. The Runners say that no one would have the courage to do this on his own. By running together, each member of the group is swept along by the others, encouraged by the screams, whipped to a frenzy of self-punishing endurance. That is the irony. In order to kill yourself by running, you first have to train yourself to be a good runner. Otherwise, you would not have the strength to push yourself far enough. The Runners, however, go through arduous preparations to meet their fate, and if they happen to fall on their way to that fate, they know how to pick themselves up immediately and continue. I suppose it's a kind of religion. There are several offices throughout the city—one for each of the nine census zones—and in order to join, you must go through a series of difficult initiations: holding your breath under water, fasting, putting your hand in the flame of a candle, not speaking to anyone for seven days. Once you have been accepted, you must submit to the code of the group. This involves six to twelve months of communal living, a strict regimen of exercise and training, and a gradually reduced intake of food. By the time a member is ready to make his death run, he has simultaneously reached a point of ultimate strength and ultimate weakness. He can theoretically run forever, and at the same time his body has used up all its resources. This combination produces the desired result. You set out with your companions on the morning of the appointed day and run until you have escaped your body, running and screaming until you have flown out of yourself. Eventually, your soul wriggles free, your body drops to the ground, and you are dead. The

12

Runners advertise that their method is over ninety percent failure-proof—which means that almost no one ever has to make a second death run.

More common are the solitary deaths. But these, too, have been transformed into a kind of public ritual. People climb to the highest places for no other reason than to jump. The Last Leap, it is called, and I admit there is something stirring about watching one, something that seems to open a whole new world of freedom inside you: to see the body poised at the roof's edge, and then, always, the slight moment of hesitation, as if from a desire to relish those final seconds, and the way your own life seems to gather in your throat, and then, unexpectedly (for you can never be sure when it will happen), the body hurls itself through the air and comes flying down to the street. You would be amazed at the enthusiasm of the crowds: to hear their frantic cheering, to see their excitement. It is as if the violence and beauty of the spectacle had wrenched them from themselves, had made them forget the paltriness of their own lives. The Last Leap is something everyone can understand, and it corresponds to everyone's inner longings: to die in a flash, to obliterate yourself in one brief and glorious moment. I sometimes think that death is the one thing we have any feeling for. It is our art form, the only way we can express ourselves.

Still, there are those of us who manage to live. For death, too, has become a source of life. With so many people thinking of how to put an end to things, meditating on the various ways to leave this world, you can imagine the opportunities for turning a profit. A clever person can live quite well off the deaths of others. For not everyone has the courage of the Runners or the Leapers, and many need to be helped along with their decision. The ability to pay for these services is naturally a precondition, and for that reason few but the wealthiest people can afford them. But business is nevertheless quite brisk, especially at the Euthanasia Clinics. These come in several different varieties, depending on how much you are willing to spend. The simplest and cheapest form takes no more than an hour or two, and it is advertised as the Return Voyage. You sign in at the Clinic, pay for your ticket at the desk, and then are taken to a small private room with a freshly made bed. An attendant tucks you in and gives you an injection, and then you drift off to sleep and never wake up. Next on the price ladder is the Journey of Marvels, which lasts anywhere from one to three days. This consists of a series of injections, spaced out at regular intervals, which gives the customer a euphoric sense of abandon and happiness, before a last, fatal injection is administered. Then there is the Pleasure Cruise, which can go on for as long as two weeks. The customers are treated to an opulent life, catered to in a manner that rivals the splendor of the old luxury hotels. There are elaborate meals, wines, entertainment, even a brothel, which serves the needs of both men and women. This runs into quite a bit of money, but for some people the chance to live the good life, even for a short while, is an irresistible temptation.

The Euthanasia Clinics are not the only way to buy your own death, however. There are the Assassination Clubs as well, and these have been growing in popularity. A person who wants to die, but who is too afraid to go through with it himself, joins the Assassination Club in his census zone for a relatively modest fee. An assassin is

14

then assigned to him. The customer is told nothing about the arrangements, and everything about his death remains a mystery to him: the date, the place, the method to be used, the identity of his assassin. In some sense, life goes on as it always has. Death remains on the horizon, an absolute certainty, and yet inscrutable as to its specific form. Instead of old age, disease, or accident, a member of an Assassination Club can look forward to a quick and violent death in the not-too-distant future: a bullet in the brain, a knife in the back, a pair of hands around his throat in the middle of the night. The effect of all this, it seems to me, is to make one more vigilant. Death is no longer an abstraction, but a real possibility that haunts each moment of life. Rather than submit passively to the inevitable, those marked for assassination tend to become more alert, more vigorous in their movements, more filled with a sense of life—as though transformed by some new understanding of things. Many of them actually recant and opt for life again. But that is a complicated business. For once you join an Assassination Club, you are not allowed to quit. On the other hand, if you manage to kill your assassin, you can be released from your obligation—and, if you choose, be hired as an assassin yourself. That is the danger of the assassin's job and the reason why it is so well paid. It is rare for an assassin to be killed, for he is necessarily more experienced than his intended victim, but it does sometimes happen. Among the poor, especially poor young men, there are many who save up for months and even years just to be able to join an Assassination Club. The idea is to get hired as an assassin—and therefore to lift themselves up to a better life. Few ever make it. If I told you the stories of some of these boys, you would not be able to sleep for a week.

All this leads to a great many practical problems. The question of bodies, for example. People don't die here as they did in the old days, quietly expiring in their beds or in the clean sanctuary of a hospital ward—they die wherever they happen to be, and for the most part that means the street. I am not just talking about the Runners, the Leapers, and members of the Assassination Clubs (for they amount to a mere fraction), but to vast segments of the population. Fully half the people are homeless, and they have absolutely nowhere to go. Dead bodies are therefore everywhere you turn—on the sidewalk, in doorways, in the street itself. Don't ask me to give you the details. It's enough for me to say it—even more than enough. No matter what you might think, the real problem is never a lack of pity. Nothing breaks here more readily than the heart.

Most of the bodies are naked. Scavengers roam the streets at all times, and it is never very long before a dead person is stripped of his belongings. First to go are the shoes, for these are in great demand and very hard to find. The pockets are next to attract attention, but usually it is just everything after that, the clothes and whatever they contain. Last come the men with chisels and pliers, who wrench the gold and silver teeth from the mouth. Because there is no escaping this fact, many families take care of the stripping themselves, not wanting to leave it to strangers. In some cases, it comes from a desire to preserve the dignity of the loved one; in others it is simply a question of selfishness. But that is perhaps too subtle a point. If the gold from your husband's tooth can feed you for a month, who is to say you are wrong to pull it out? This kind of behavior goes against the grain, I know, but if you mean to survive here, then you must be able to give in on matters of principle.

Every morning, the city sends out trucks to collect the corpses. This is the chief function of the government, and more money is spent on it than anything else. All around the edges of the city are the crematoria—the so-called Transformation Centers—and day and night you can see the smoke rising up into the sky. But with the streets in such bad repair now, and with so many of them reduced to rubble, the job becomes increasingly difficult. The men are forced to stop the trucks and go out foraging on foot, and this slows down the work considerably. On top of this, there are the frequent mechanical breakdowns of the trucks and the occasional outbursts from onlookers. Throwing stones at death-truck workers is a common occupation among the homeless. Although the workers are armed and have been known to turn their machine guns on crowds, some of the stone-throwers are very deft at hiding themselves, and their hit-and-run tactics can sometimes bring the collection work to a complete halt. There is no coherent motive behind these attacks. They stem from anger, resentment, and boredom, and because the collection workers are the only city officials who ever make an appearance in the neighborhood, they are convenient targets. One could say that the stones represent the people's disgust with a government that does nothing for them until they are dead. But that would be going too far. The stones are an expression of unhappiness, and that is all. For there are no politics in the city as such. The people are too hungry, too distracted, too much at odds with each other for that.

The crossing took ten days, and I was the only passenger. But you know that already. You met the captain and the crew, you saw my cabin, and there's no need to go over that again. I spent my time looking at the water and the sky and hardly opened a book for the whole ten days. We came into the city at night, and it was only then that I began to panic a little. The shore was entirely black, no lights anywhere, and it felt as though we were entering an invisible world, a place where only blind people lived. But I had the address of William's office, and that reassured me somewhat. All I had to do was go there, I thought, and then things would take care of themselves. At the very least, I felt confident that I would be able to pick up William's trail. But I had not realized that the street would be gone. It wasn't that the office was empty or that the building had been abandoned. There was no building, no street, no anything at all: nothing but stones and rubbish for acres around.

This was the third census zone, I later learned, and nearly a year before some kind of epidemic had broken out there. The city government had come in, walled off the area, and burned everything down to the ground. Or so the story went. I have since learned not to take the things I am told too seriously. It's not that people make a point of lying to you, it's just that where the past is concerned, the truth tends to get obscured rather quickly. Legends crop up within a matter of hours, tall tales circulate, and the facts are soon buried under a mountain of outlandish theories. In the city, the best approach is to believe only what your own eyes tell you. But not even that is infallible. For few things are ever what they seem to be, especially here, with so much to absorb at every step, with so many things that defy understanding. Whatever you see has the potential to wound you, to make you less than you are, as if merely by seeing a thing some part of yourself were taken away from you. Often, you feel it will be dangerous to look, and there is a tendency to avert your eyes, or even to shut them. Because of that, it is easy to get confused, to be unsure that you are really seeing the thing you think you are looking at. It could be that you are imagining it, or mixing it up with something else, or remembering something you have seen before—or perhaps even imagined before. You see how complicated it is. It is not enough simply to look and say to yourself, "I am looking at that thing." For it is one thing to do this when the object before your eyes is a pencil, say, or a crust of bread. But what happens when you find yourself looking at a dead child, at a little girl lying in the street without any clothes on, her head crushed and covered with blood? What do you say to yourself then? It is not a simple matter, you see, to state flatly and without equivocation: "I am looking at a dead child." Your mind seems to balk at forming the words, you somehow cannot bring yourself to do it. For the thing before your eyes is not something you can very easily separate from yourself. That is what I mean by being wounded: you cannot merely see, for each thing somehow belongs to you, is part of the story unfolding inside you. It would be good, I suppose, to make yourself so hard that nothing could affect you anymore. But then you would be alone, so totally cut off from everyone else that life would become impossible. There are those who manage to do this here, who find the strength to turn themselves into monsters, but you would be surprised to know how few they are. Or, to put it another way: we have all become monsters, but there is almost no one without some remnant inside him of life as it once was.

That is perhaps the greatest problem of all. Life as we know it has ended, and yet no one is able to grasp what has taken its place. Those of us who were brought up somewhere else, or who are old enough to remember a world different from this one, find it an enormous struggle just to keep up from one day to the next. I am not talking only of hardships. Faced with the most ordinary occurrence, you no longer know how to act, and because you cannot act, you find yourself unable to think. The brain is in a muddle. All around you one change follows another, each day produces a new upheaval, the old assumptions are so much air and emptiness. That is the dilemma. On the one hand, you want to survive, to adapt, to make the best of things as they are. But, on the other hand, to accomplish this seems to entail killing off all those things that once made you think of yourself as human. Do you see what I am trying to say? In order to live, you must make yourself die. That is why so many people have given up. For no matter how hard they struggle, they know they are bound to lose. And at that point it is surely a pointless thing to struggle at all.

It tends to blur in my mind now: what happened and did not, the streets for the first time, the days, the nights, the sky above me, the stones stretching beyond. I seem to remember looking up a lot, as if searching the sky for some lack, some surplus, some thing that made it different from other skies, as if the sky could explain the things I was seeing around me. I could be mistaken, however. Possibly

I am transferring the observations of a later period onto those first days. But I doubt that it matters very much, least of all now.

After much careful study, I can safely report that the sky here is the same sky as the one above you. We have the same clouds and the same brightnesses, the same storms and the same calms, the same winds that carry everything along with them. If the effects are somewhat different here, that is strictly because of what happens below. The nights, for example, are never quite what they are at home. There is the same darkness and the same immensity, but with no feeling of stillness, only a constant undertow, a murmur that pulls you downward and thrusts you forward, without respite. And then, during the days, there is a brightness that is sometimes intolerable—a brilliance that stuns you and seems to blanch everything, all the jagged surfaces gleaming, the air itself almost a shimmer. The light forms in such a way that the colors become more and more distorted as you draw close to them. Even the shadows are agitated, with a random, hectic pulsing along the edges. You must be careful in this light not to open your eyes too wide, to squint at just the precise degree that will allow you to keep your balance. Otherwise, you will stumble as you walk, and I need not enumerate the dangers of falling. If not for the darkness, and the strange nights that descend on us, I sometimes feel the sky would burn itself out. The days end when they must, at just the moment when the sun seems to have exhausted the things it shines on. Nothing could adhere to the brightness anymore. The whole implausible world would melt away, and that would be that.

Slowly and steadily, the city seems to be consuming itself, even as it remains. There is no way to explain it. I can only record, I cannot pretend to understand. Every day in the streets you hear explosions, as if somewhere far from you a building were falling down or the sidewalk caving in. But you never see it happen. No matter how often you hear these sounds, their source remains invisible. You would think that now and then an explosion would take place in your presence. But the facts fly in the face of probability. You mustn't think that I am making it up—these noises do not begin in my head. The others hear them too, even if they don't pay much attention. Sometimes they will stop to comment on them, but they never seem worried. It's a bit better now, they might say. Or, it seems somewhat belligerent this afternoon. I used to ask many questions about these explosions, but I never got an answer. Nothing more than a dumb stare or a shrug of the shoulders. Eventually, I learned that some things are just not asked, that even here there are subjects no one is willing to discuss.

For those at the bottom, there are the streets and the parks and the old subway stations. The streets are the worst, for there you are exposed to every hazard and inconvenience. The parks are a somewhat more settled affair, without the problem of traffic and constant passersby, but unless you are one of the fortunate ones to have a tent or a hut, you are never free of the weather. Only in the subway stations can you be sure to escape inclemencies, but there you are also forced to contend with a host of other irritations: the dampness, the crowds, and the perpetual noise of people shouting, as though mesmerized by the echoes of their own voices.

During those first weeks, it was the rain I came to fear more than anything else. Even the cold is a trifle by comparison. For that, it is simply a question of a warm coat (which I had) and moving briskly to keep the blood stimulated. I also learned the benefits to be found from newspapers, surely the best and cheapest material for insulating your clothes. On cold days, you must get up very early in the morning to be sure of finding a good place in the lines that gather in front of the newsstands. You must gauge the wait judiciously, for there is nothing worse than standing out in the cold morning air too long. If you think you will be there for more than twenty or twenty-five minutes, then the common wisdom is to move on and forget it.

Once you've bought the paper, assuming you've managed to get one, the best thing is to take a sheet, tear it into strips, and then twist them into little bundles. These knots are good for stuffing into the toes of your shoes, for blocking up windy interstices around your ankles, and for threading through holes in your clothing. For the limbs and torso, whole sheets wrapped around a number of loosely fitting knots is often the best procedure. For the neck area, it is good to take a dozen or so knots and braid them together into a collar. The whole thing gives you a puffy, padded look, which has the cosmetic advantage of disguising thinness. For those who are concerned about keeping up appearances, the "paper meal," as it is called, serves as a kind of face-saving technique. People literally starving to death, with caved-in stomachs and limbs like sticks, walk around trying to look as though they weigh two or three hundred pounds. No one is ever fooled by this disguise—you can spot these people from half a mile off—but perhaps that is not the real point. What they seem to be saying is that they know what has happened to them, and they are ashamed of it. More than anything else, their bulked-up bodies are a badge of consciousness, a sign of bitter self-awareness. They turn themselves into grotesque parodies of the prosperous and well-fed, and in this frustrated, half-crazed stab at respectability, they prove they are just the opposite of what they pretend to be—and that they know it.

The rain, however, is unconquerable. For once you get wet, you go on paying for it hours and even days afterward. There is no greater mistake than getting caught in a downpour. Not only do you run the risk of a cold, but you must suffer through innumerable discomforts: your clothes saturated with dampness, your bones as though frozen, and the ever-present danger of destroying your shoes. If staying on your feet is the single most important task, then imagine the consequences of having less than adequate shoes. And nothing affects shoes more disastrously than a good soaking. This can lead to all kinds of problems: blisters, bunions, corns, ingrown toenails, sores, malformations—and when walking becomes painful, you are as good as lost. One step and then another step and then another: that is the golden rule. If you cannot bring yourself to do even that, then you might as well just lie down right then and there and tell yourself to stop breathing.

But how to avoid the rain if it can strike at any moment? There are times, many times, when you find yourself outdoors, going from one place to another, on your way somewhere with no choice about it, and suddenly the sky grows dark, the clouds collide, and there you are, drenched to the skin. And even if you manage to find shelter the moment the rain begins to fall and to spare yourself this once, you still must be extremely careful after the rain stops. For then you must watch for the puddles that form in the hollows of the pavement, the lakes that sometimes emerge from the rifts, and even the mud that oozes up from below, ankle-deep and treacherous. With the streets in such poor repair, with so much that is cracked, pitted, pocked, and riven apart, there is no escaping these crises. Sooner or later, you are bound to come to a place where you have no alternative, where you are hemmed in on all sides. And not only are there the surfaces to watch for, the world that touches your feet, there are the drippings from above as well, the water that slides down from the eaves, and then, even worse, the strong winds that often follow the rain, the fierce eddies of air, skimming the tops of lakes and puddles and whipping the water back into the atmosphere, driving it along like little pins, darts that prick your face and swirl around you, making it impossible to see anything at all. When the winds blow after a rain, people collide with one another more frequently, more fights break out in the streets, the very air seems charged with menace.

It would be one thing if the weather could be predicted with any degree of accuracy. Then one could make plans, know when to avoid the streets, prepare for changes in advance. But everything happens too fast here, the shifts are too abrupt, what is true one minute is no longer true the next. I have wasted much time looking for signs in the air, trying to study the atmosphere for hints of what is to follow and when: the color and heft of the clouds, the speed and direction of the wind, the smells at any given hour, the texture of the sky at night, the sprawl of the sunsets, the intensity of the dew at dawn. But nothing has ever helped me. To correlate this with that, to make a connection between an afternoon cloud and an evening wind—such things lead only to madness. You spin around in the vortex of your calculations and then, just at the moment you are convinced it will rain, the sun goes on shining for an entire day.

What you must do, then, is be prepared for anything. But opinions vary drastically on the best way to go about this. There is a small minority, for example, that believes that bad weather comes from bad thoughts. This is a rather mystical approach to the question, for it implies that thoughts can be translated directly into events in the physical world. According to them, when you think a dark or pessimistic thought, it produces a cloud in the sky. If enough people are thinking gloomy thoughts at once, then rain will begin to fall. That is the reason for all the startling shifts in the weather, they claim, and the reason why no one has been able to give a scientific explanation of our bizarre climate. Their solution is to maintain a steadfast cheerfulness, no matter how dismal the conditions around them. No frowns, no deep sighs, no tears. These people are known as the Smilers, and no sect in the city is more innocent or childlike. If a majority of the population could be converted to their beliefs, they are convinced the weather would at last begin to stabilize and that life would then improve. They are therefore always proselytizing, continually looking for new adherents, but the mildness of the manner they have imposed on themselves makes them feeble persuaders. They rarely succeed in winning anyone over, and consequently their ideas have never been put to the test—for without a great number of believers, there will not be enough good thoughts to make a difference. But this lack of proof only makes them more stubborn in their faith. I

26

can see you shaking your head, and yes, I agree with you that these people are ridiculous and misguided. But, in the day-to-day context of the city, there is a certain force to their argument—and it is probably no more absurd than any other. As people, the Smilers tend to be refreshing company, for their gentleness and optimism are a welcome antidote to the angry bitterness you find everywhere else.

By contrast, there is another group called the Crawlers. These people believe that conditions will go on worsening until we demonstrate—in an utterly persuasive manner—how ashamed we are of how we lived in the past. Their solution is to prostrate themselves on the ground and refuse to stand up again until some sign is given to them that their penance has been deemed sufficient. What this sign is supposed to be is the subject of long theoretical debates. Some say a month of rain, others say a month of fair weather, and still others say they will not know until it is revealed to them in their hearts. There are two principal factions in this sect—the Dogs and the Snakes. The first contend that crawling on hands and knees shows adequate contrition, whereas the second hold that nothing short of moving on one's belly is good enough. Bloody fights often break out between the two groups—each vying for control of the other—but neither faction has gained much of a following, and by now I believe the sect is on the verge of dying out.

In the end, most people have no fixed opinion about these questions. If I counted up the various groups that have a coherent theory about the weather (the Drummers, the End-of-the-Worlders, the Free Associationists), I doubt they would come to more than a drop in the bucket. What it boils down to mostly, I think, is pure luck. The sky is ruled by chance, by forces so complex and obscure that no one can fully explain it. If you happen to get wet in the rain, you are unlucky, and that's all there is to it. If you happen to stay dry, then so much the better. But it has nothing to do with your attitudes or your beliefs. The rain makes no distinctions. At one time or another, it falls on everyone, and when it falls, everyone is equal to everyone else—no one better, no one worse, everyone equal and the same.

There is so much I want to tell you. Then I begin to say something, and I suddenly realize how little I understand. Facts and figures, I mean, precise information about how we live here in the city. That was going to be William's job. The newspaper sent him here to get the story, and every week there was going to be another report. Historical background, human interest articles, the whole business. But we didn't get much, did we? A few short dispatches and then silence. If William couldn't manage it, I don't see how I can expect myself to do any better. I have no idea how the city keeps itself going, and even if I were to investigate these matters, it would probably take so long that the entire situation would have changed by the time I found out. Where vegetables are grown, for example, and how they are transported to the city. I can't give you the answers, and I have never met anyone who could. People talk about agricultural zones in the hinterlands to the west, but that doesn't mean there is any truth to it. People will talk about anything here, especially things they know nothing about. What strikes me as odd is not that everything is falling apart, but that so much continues to be there. It takes a long time for a world to vanish, much longer than you

28

would think. Lives continue to be lived, and each one of us remains the witness of his own little drama. It's true that there are no schools anymore; it's true that the last movie was shown over five years ago; it's true that wine is so scarce now that only the rich can afford it. But is that what we mean by life? Let everything fall away, and then let's see what there is. Perhaps that is the most interesting question of all: to see what happens when there is nothing, and whether or not we will survive that too.

The consequences can be rather curious, and they often go against your expectations. Utter despair can exist side by side with the most dazzling invention; entropy and efflorescence merge. Because there is so little left, almost nothing gets thrown out anymore, and uses have been found for materials that were once scorned as rubbish. It all has to do with a new way of thinking. Scarcity bends your mind toward novel solutions, and you discover yourself willing to entertain ideas that never would have occurred to you before. Take the subject of human waste, literal human waste. Plumbing hardly exists here anymore. Pipes have corroded, toilets have cracked and sprung leaks, the sewer system is largely defunct. Rather than have people fend for themselves and dispose of their slops in some hodgepodge manner—which would quickly lead to chaos and disease—an elaborate system was devised whereby each neighborhood is patrolled by a team of night soil collectors. They rumble through the streets three times a day, lugging and pushing their rusty engines over the split pavement, clanging their bells for the neighborhood people to come outside and empty their buckets into the tank. The odor is of course overpowering, and when this system was first installed the only people willing to do the work were prisoners—who were given the dubious choice of receiving an extended sentence if they refused and a shorter sentence if they agreed. Things have changed since then, however, and the Fecalists now have the status of civil servants and are provided with housing on a par with that given to the police. It seems only right, I suppose. If there were not some advantage to be gained from this work, why would anyone want to do it? It only goes to show how effective the government can be under certain circumstances. Dead bodies and shit— when it comes to removing health hazards, our administrators are positively Roman in their organization, a model of clear thinking and efficiency.

It doesn't end there, however. Once the Fecalists have collected the waste, they do not simply dispose of it. Shit and garbage have become crucial resources here, and with the stocks of coal and oil having dwindled to dangerously low levels, they are the things that supply us with much of the energy we are still able to produce. Each census zone has its own power plant, and these are run entirely on waste. Fuel for running cars, fuel for heating houses—all this comes from the methane gas created in these plants. It might sound funny to you, I realize, but no one jokes about it here. Shit is a serious business, and anyone caught dumping it in the streets is arrested. With your second offense, you are automatically given the death penalty. A system like that tends to dampen your playfulness. You go along with what is demanded of you, and pretty soon you don't even think about it anymore.

The essential thing is to survive. If you mean to last here, you must have a way of earning money, and yet there are few jobs left in the old sense of the word. Without connections, you cannot apply for even the humblest government position (clerk, janitor, Transformation Center employee, and so on). The same holds true for the various legal and illegal businesses around the city (the Euthanasia Clinics, the renegade food operations, the phantom landlords). Unless you already know someone, it is pointless to ask any of these people for work. For those at the bottom, therefore, scavenging is the most common solution. This is the job for people with no job, and my guess is that a good ten to twenty percent of the population is engaged in it. I did it myself for a while, and the facts are very simple: once you begin, it is nearly impossible to stop. It takes so much out of you, there is no time left to think of doing anything else.

All scavengers fall into one of two basic categories: garbage collectors and object hunters. The first group is considerably larger than the second, and if one works hard, diligently sticking to it twelve or fourteen hours a day, there is an even chance of making a living. For many years now, there has been no municipal garbage system. Instead, the city is divided up by a number of private garbage brokers—one for each census zone—who purchased the rights from the city government to collect garbage in their areas. To get work as a garbage collector you must first obtain a permit from one of the brokers—for which you must pay a monthly fee, sometimes as much as fifty percent of your earnings. To work without a permit is tempting, but it is also extremely dangerous, for each broker has his own crew of inspectors to patrol the streets, making spot checks on anyone they see collecting garbage. If you can't produce the proper papers, the inspectors have the legal right to fine you, and if you can't pay the fine, you are arrested. That means deportation to one of the labor camps west of the city—and spending the next seven years in prison. Some people say that life in the camps is better than it is in the city, but that is only speculation. A few have even gone so far as to get themselves arrested on purpose, but no one has ever seen them again.

Assuming that you are a duly registered garbage collector and that all your papers are in order, you earn your money by gathering up as much as you can and taking it to the nearest power plant. There you are paid so much money per pound—a trivial amount—and the garbage is then dumped into one of the processing tanks. The preferred instrument for transporting garbage is the shopping cart—similar to the ones we have back home. These metal baskets on wheels have proved to be sturdy objects, and there is no question that they work more efficiently than anything else. A larger vehicle would become too exhausting to push when filled to capacity, and a smaller one would require too many trips to the depot. (A pamphlet was even published on this subject a few years back, which proved the accuracy of these assumptions.) As a consequence, these carts are in great demand, and the first goal of every new garbage collector is to be able to afford one. This can take months, sometimes even years—but until you have a cart, it is impossible to make a go of it. There is a deadly equation buried in all this. Since the work brings in so little, you rarely have a chance to put anything aside—and if you do, that usually means you are depriving yourself of something essential: food, for example, without which you will not have the strength to do the work necessary to earn the money to buy the cart. You see the problem. The harder you work, the weaker you become; the weaker you are, the more draining the work. But that is only the beginning. For even if you manage to obtain a cart, you must be vigilant about keeping it in good repair. The streets are murderous on equipment, and the wheels in particular must be attended to with constant watchfulness. But even if you manage to stay on top of these matters, there is the additional obligation of never letting the cart out of your sight. Since the carts have become so valuable, they are especially coveted by thieves—and no calamity could be more tragic than losing your cart. Most scavengers therefore invest in some kind of tether device known as an "umbilical cord"—meaning a rope, or a dog leash, or a chain, which you literally tie around your waist and then attach to the cart. This makes walking a cumbersome business, but it is worth the trouble. Because of the noise these chains make as the cart goes bumping along the street, scavengers are often referred to as "musicians."

An object hunter must go through the same registration procedures as a garbage collector and is subject to the same random inspections, but his work is of a different kind. The garbage collector looks for waste; the object hunter looks for salvage. He is in search of specific goods and materials that can be used again, and though he is free to do whatever he likes with the objects he finds, he generally sells them to one of the Resurrection Agents around the city—private entrepreneurs who convert these odds and ends into new goods that are eventually sold on the open market. The Agents perform a multiple function—part junk dealer, part manufacturer, part shopkeeper—and with other modes of production in the city now nearly extinct, they are among the richest and most powerful people around, rivaled only by the garbage brokers themselves. A good object hunter, therefore, can stand to make an acceptable living from his work. But you must be quick, you must be clever, and you must know where to look. Young people tend to do best at it, and it is rare to see an object hunter who is over twenty or twenty-five. Those who cannot make the grade must soon look for other work, for there is no guarantee that you will get anything for your efforts. Garbage collectors are an older and more conservative lot, content to toil away at their jobs because they know it will provide them with a living—at least if they work as hard as they can. But nothing is really sure, for the competition has become terrible at all levels of scavenging. The scarcer things become in the city, the more reluctant people are to throw anything out. Whereas previously you would not think twice about tossing an orange rind onto the street, now even the rinds are ground up into mush and eaten by many people. A frayed T-shirt, a pair of torn underpants, the brim of a hat—all these things are now saved, to be patched together into a new set of clothes. You see people dressed in the most motley and bizarre costumes, and each time some patchwork person walks by, you know that he has probably put another object hunter out of work.

Nevertheless, that is what I went in for—object hunting. I was lucky enough to begin before my money ran out. Even after I bought the license (seventeen glots), the cart (sixty-six glots), a leash and a new pair of shoes (five glots and seventy-one glots), I still had more than two hundred glots left over. This was fortunate, for it gave me a certain margin of error, and at that point I needed all the help I could get. Sooner or later, it would be sink or swim—but for the moment I had something to hold on to: a piece of floating wood, a chunk of flotsam to bear my weight.

In the beginning, it did not go well. The city was new for me back then, and I always seemed to be lost. I squandered time on forays that yielded nothing, bad hunches on barren streets, being in the wrong spot at the wrong time. If I happened to find something, it was always because I had stumbled onto it by accident. Chance was my only approach, the purely gratuitous act of seeing a thing with my own two eyes and then bending down to pick it up. I had no method as the others seemed to have, no way of knowing in advance where to go, no sense of what would be where and when. It takes years of living in the city to get to that point, and I was only a novice, an ignorant newcomer who could barely find her way from one census zone to the next.

Still, I was not a total failure. I had my legs, after all, and a certain youthful enthusiasm to keep me going, even when the prospects were less than encouraging. I scampered around in breathless surges, dodging the dangerous byways and toll mounds, careening fitfully from one street to another, never failing to hope for some extraordinary find around the next corner. It is an odd thing, I believe, to be constantly looking down at the ground, always searching for broken and discarded things. After a while, it must surely affect the brain. For nothing is really itself anymore. There are pieces of this and pieces of that, but none of it fits together. And yet, very strangely, at the limit of all this chaos, everything begins to fuse again. A pulverized apple and a pulverized orange are finally the same thing, aren't they? You can't tell the difference between a good dress and a bad dress if they're both torn to shreds, can you? At a certain point, things disintegrate into muck, or dust, or scraps, and what you have is something new, some particle or agglomeration of matter that cannot be identified. It is a clump, a mote, a fragment of the world that has no place: a cipher of it-ness. As an object hunter, you must rescue things before they reach this state of absolute decay. You can never expect to find something whole—for that is an accident, a mistake on the part of the person who lost it—but neither can you spend your time looking for what is totally used up. You hover somewhere in between, on the lookout for things that still retain a semblance of their original shape—even if their usefulness is gone. What another has seen fit to throw away, you must examine, dissect, and bring back to life. A piece of string, a bottle-cap, an undamaged board from a bashed-in crate—none of these things should be neglected. Everything falls apart, but not every part of every thing, at least not at the same time. The job is to zero in on these little islands of intactness, to imagine them joined to other such islands, and those islands to still others, and thus to create new archipelagoes of matter. You must salvage the salvageable and learn to ignore the rest. The trick is to do it as fast as you can.

Little by little, my hauls became almost adequate. Odds and ends, of course, but a few totally unexpected things as well: a collapsible telescope with one cracked lens; a rubber Frankenstein mask; a bicycle wheel; a Cyrillic typewriter missing only five keys and the space bar; the passport of a man named Quinn. These treasures made up for some of the bad days, and as time went on I began doing well enough at the Resurrection Agents' to leave my nest egg untouched. I might have done better, I think, but there were certain lines I drew within myself, limits I refused to step beyond. Touching the dead, for example. Stripping corpses is one of the most profitable aspects of scavenging, and there are few object hunters who do not pounce at the chance. I kept telling myself that I was a fool, a squeamish little rich girl who didn't want to live, but nothing really helped. I tried. Once or twice I even got close—but when it came right down to it, I didn't have the courage. I remember an old man and an adolescent girl: crouching down beside them, letting my hands get near their bodies, trying to convince myself that it didn't matter. And then, on Lampshade Road one day, early in the morning, a small boy of about six. I just couldn't bring myself to do it. It's not that I felt proud of myself for having made some deep moral decision—I just didn't have it in me to go that far.

Another thing that hurt me was that I stuck to myself. I didn't mix with other scavengers, made no effort to become friends with anyone. You need allies, however, especially to protect yourself against the Vultures—scavengers who make their living by stealing from other scavengers. The inspectors turn their backs on this nastiness, concentrating their attention on those who scavenge without a license. For bona fide scavengers, therefore, the job is a free-for-all, with constant attacks and counterattacks, a sense that anything can happen to you at any time. My hauls were filched on the average of about once a week, and it got so that I began to calculate these losses in advance, as though they were a normal part of the work. With friends, I might have been able to avoid some of these raids. But in the long run it did not seem worth it to me. The scavengers were a repulsive bunch—Vultures and non-Vultures alike—and it turned my stomach to listen to their schemes, their boasting, and their lies. The important thing was that I never lost my cart. Those were my early days

37

in the city, and I was still strong enough to hold on to it, still quick enough to dart away from danger whenever I had to.

Bear with me. I know that I sometimes stray from the point, but unless I write down things as they occur to me, I feel I will lose them for good. My mind is not quite what it used to be. It is slower now, sluggish and less nimble, and to follow even the simplest thought very far exhausts me. This is how it begins, then, in spite of my efforts. The words come only when I think I won't be able to find them anymore, at the moment I despair of ever bringing them out again. Each day brings the same struggle, the same blankness, the same desire to forget and then not to forget. When it begins, it is never anywhere but here, never anywhere but at this limit that the pencil begins to write. The story starts and stops, goes forward and then loses itself, and between each word, what silences, what words escape and vanish, never to be seen again.

For a long time I tried not to remember anything. By confining my thoughts to the present, I was better able to manage, better able to avoid the sulks. Memory is the great trap, you see, and I did my best to hold myself back, to make sure my thoughts did not sneak off to the old days. But lately I have been slipping, a little more each day it seems, and now there are times when I will not let go: of my parents, of William, of you. I was such a wild young thing, wasn't I? I grew up too fast for my own good, and no one could tell me anything I didn't already know. Now I can think only of how I hurt my parents, and how my mother cried when I told her I was leaving. It wasn't enough

38

that they had already lost William, now they were going to lose me as well. Please—if you see my parents, tell them I'm sorry. I need to know that someone will do that for me, and there's no one to count on but you.

Yes, there are many things I'm ashamed of. At times my life seems nothing but a series of regrets, of wrong turnings, of irreversible mistakes. That is the problem when you begin to look back. You see yourself as you were, and you are appalled. But it's too late for apologies now, I realize that. It's too late for anything but getting on with it. These are the words, then. Sooner or later, I will try to say everything, and it makes no difference what comes when, whether the first thing is the second thing or the second thing the last. It all swirls around in my head at once, and merely to hold on to a thing long enough to say it is a victory. If this confuses you, I'm sorry. But I don't have much choice. I have to take it strictly as I can get it.

I never found William, she continued. Perhaps that goes without saying. I never found him, and I never met anyone who could tell me where he was. Reason tells me he is dead, but I can't be certain of it. There is no evidence to support even the wildest guess, and until I have some proof, I prefer to keep an open mind. Without knowledge, one can neither hope nor despair. The best one can do is doubt, and under the circumstances doubt is a great blessing.

Even if William is not in the city, he could be somewhere else. This country is enormous, you understand, and there's no telling where he might have gone. Beyond the agricultural zone to the west, there are supposedly several hundred miles of desert. Beyond that, however, one hears talk of more cities, of mountain ranges, of mines and factories, of vast territories stretching all the way to a second ocean. Perhaps there is some truth to this talk. If so, William might well have tried his luck in one of those places. I am not forgetting how difficult it is to leave the city, but we both know what William was like. If there was the slightest possibility of getting out, he would have found a way.

I never told you this, but some time during my last week at home, I met with the editor of William's newspaper. It must have been three or four days before I said good-bye to you, and I avoided mentioning it because I did not want us to have another argument. Things were bad enough as they were, and it only would have spoiled those last moments we had together. Don't be angry with me now, I beg you. I don't think I could stand it.

The editor's name was Bogat—a bald, big-bellied man with old-fashioned suspenders and a watch in his fob pocket. He made me think of my grandfather: overworked, licking the tips of his pencils before he wrote, exuding an air of abstracted benevolence that seemed tinged with cunning, a pleasantness that masked some secret edge of cruelty. I waited nearly an hour in the reception room. When he was finally ready to see me, he led me by the elbow into his office, sat me down in his chair, and listened to my story. I must have talked for five or ten minutes before he interrupted me. William had not sent a dispatch for over nine months, he said. Yes, he understood that the machines were broken in the city, but that was beside the point. A good reporter always manages to file his story—and William had been his best man. A silence of nine months could only mean one thing: William had run into trouble, and he would not be coming back. Very blunt, no beating around the bush. I shrugged my shoulders and told him that he was only guessing.

"Don't do it, little girl," he said. "You'd be crazy to go there."

"I'm not a little girl," I said. "I'm nineteen years old, and I can take care of myself better than you think."

"I don't care if you're a hundred. No one gets out of there. It's the end of the goddamned world."

I knew he was right. But I had made up my mind, and nothing was going to force me to change it. Seeing my stubbornness, Bogat began to modify his tactics.

"Look," he said, "I sent another man over there about a month ago. I should be getting word from him soon. Why not wait until then? You could get all your answers without having to leave."

"What does that have to do with my brother?"

"William is a part of the story, too. If this reporter does his job, he'll find out what happened to him."

But it wasn't going to wash, and Bogat knew it. I held my ground, determined to fend off his smug paternalism, and little by little he seemed to give up. Without my asking for it, he gave me the name of the new reporter, and then, as a last gesture, opened the drawer of a filing cabinet behind his desk and pulled out a photograph of a young man.

"Maybe you should take this along with you," he said, tossing it onto the desk. "Just in case."

It was a picture of the reporter. I gave it a brief glance and then slipped it into my bag to oblige him. That was the end of our talk. The meeting had been a standoff, with neither one of us giving in to the other. I think Bogat was both angry and a little impressed.

"Just remember that I told you so," he said.

"I won't forget," I said. "After I bring William back, I'll come in here and remind you of this conversation."

Bogat was about to say something more, but then he seemed to think better of it. He let out a sigh, slapped his palms softly against the desk, and stood up from his chair. "Don't get me wrong," he said. "I'm not against you. It's just that I think you're making a mistake. There's a difference, you know."

"Maybe there is. But it's still wrong to do nothing. People need time, and you shouldn't jump to conclusions before you know what you're talking about."

"That's the problem," Bogat said. "I know exactly what I'm talking about."

At that point I think we shook hands, or perhaps we just stared at each other across the desk. Then he walked me through the press room and out to the elevators in the hall. We waited there in silence, not even looking at each other. Bogat rocked back and forth on his heels, humming tunelessly under his breath. It was obvious that he was already thinking about something else. As the doors opened and I stepped into the elevator, he said to me wearily, "Have a nice life, little girl." Before I had a chance to answer him, the doors closed, and I was on my way down.

In the end, that photograph made all the difference. I wasn't even planning to take it with me, but then I packed it in with my things at the last minute, almost as an afterthought. At that point I didn't know that William had disappeared, of course. I had been expecting to find his replacement at the newspaper office and begin my search

42

there. But nothing went as planned. When I reached the third census zone and saw what had happened to it, I understood that this picture was suddenly the only thing I had left. It was my last link to William.

The man's name was Samuel Farr, but other than that I knew nothing about him. I had behaved too arrogantly with Bogat to ask for any details, and now I had precious little to go on. A name and a face, and that was all. With the proper sense and humility, I might have spared myself a good deal of trouble. Ultimately, I did meet up with Sam, but that had nothing to do with me. It was the work of pure chance, one of those bits of luck that fall down on you from the sky. And a long time passed before that happened—more time than I would like to remember.

The first days were the hardest. I wandered around like a sleepwalker, not knowing where I was, not even daring to talk to anyone. At one point I sold my bags to a Resurrection Agent, and that kept me in food for an ample stretch, but even after I began working as a scavenger, I had no place to live. I slept outside in all kinds of weather, hunting for a different place to sleep every night. God knows how long this period lasted, but there's no question that it was the worst, the one that came closest to doing me in. Two or three weeks minimum, perhaps as long as several months. I was so miserable that my mind seemed to stop working. I became dull inside, all instinct and selfishness. Terrible things happened to me then, and I still don't know how I managed to live through it. I was nearly raped by a Tollist on the corner of Dictionary Place and Muldoon Boulevard. I stole food from an old man who tried to rob me one night in the atrium of the old Hypnotists' Theatre— snatched the porridge right out of his hands and didn't even feel sorry about it. I had no friends, no one to talk to, no one to share a meal with. If not for the picture of Sam, I don't think I would have made it. Just knowing that he was in the city gave me something to hope for. This is the man who will help you, I kept telling myself, and once you find him, everything will be different. I must have pulled the photograph out of my pocket a hundred times a day. After a while, it became so creased and rumpled that the face was almost obliterated. But by then I knew it by heart, and the picture itself no longer mattered. I kept it with me as an amulet, a tiny shield to ward off despair.

Then my luck changed. It must have been a month or two after I began working as an object hunter, although that is just a guess. I was walking along the outskirts of the fifth census zone one day, near the spot where Filament Square had once been, when I saw a tall, middle-aged woman pushing a shopping cart over the stones, bumping along slowly and awkwardly, her thoughts obviously not on what she was doing. The sun was bright that day, the kind of sun that dazzles you and makes things invisible, and the air was hot, I remember that, very hot, almost to the point of dizziness. Just as the woman managed to get the cart into the middle of the street, a band of Runners came charging around the corner. There were twelve or fifteen of them, and they were running at full tilt, closely packed together, screaming that ecstatic death-drone of theirs. I saw the woman look up at them, as if suddenly shaken from her reverie, but instead of scrambling out of the way, she froze to her spot, standing like a bewildered deer trapped in the headlights of a car. For some reason, and even now I don't know why I did it, I unhooked the umbilical cord from my waist, ran from where I was, grabbed hold of the woman with my two arms, and dragged her out of the way a second or two before the Runners passed. It was that close. If I hadn't done it, she probably would have been trampled to death.

That was how I met Isabel. For better or worse, my true life in the city began at that moment. Everything else is prologue, a swarm of tottering steps, of days and nights, of thought I do not remember. If not for that one irrational moment in the street, the story I am telling you would not be this one. Given the shape I was in at the time, I doubt there would have been any story at all.

We lay there panting in the gutter, still hanging on to each other. As the last of the Runners disappeared around the corner, Isabel gradually seemed to understand what had happened to her. She sat up, looked around her, looked at me, and then, very slowly, began to cry. It was a moment of horrible recognition for her. Not because she had come so close to being killed, but because she had not known where she was. I felt sorry for her, and also a little afraid. Who was this thin, trembling woman with the long face and hollow eyes—and what was I doing sprawled out next to her in the street? She seemed half out of her mind, and once I had my breath back, my first impulse was to get away.

"Oh, my dear child," she said, reaching tentatively for my face. "Oh, my dear, sweet, little child, you've cut yourself. You jump out to help an old woman, and you're the one who gets hurt. Do you know why that is? It's because I'm bad luck. Everyone knows it, but they don't have the heart to tell me. But I know. I know everything, even if no one tells me."

I had scratched myself on one of the stones as we fell,

45

and blood was trickling from my left temple. But it was nothing serious, no cause for panic. I was about to say good-bye and walk off, when I felt a little pang about leaving her. Perhaps I should take her home, I thought, to make sure that nothing else happens to her. I helped her to her feet and retrieved the shopping cart from across the square.

"Ferdinand will be furious with me," she said. "This is the third day in a row I've come up empty-handed. A few more days like this, and we'll be finished."

"I think you should go home anyway," I said. "At least for a while. You're in no condition to be pushing around this cart now."

"But Ferdinand. He'll go crazy when he sees I don't have anything."

"Don't worry," I said. "I'll explain what happened."

I had no idea what I was talking about, of course, but something had taken hold of me, and I couldn't control it: some sudden rush of pity, some stupid need to take care of this woman. Perhaps the old stories about saving someone's life are true. Once it happens, they say, that person becomes your responsibility, and whether you like it or not, the two of you belong to each other forever.

It took us nearly three hours to get back to her house. Under normal circumstances, it would have taken only half that long, but Isabel moved so slowly, walked with such faltering steps, that the sun was already going down by the time we got there. She had no umbilical cord with her (she had lost it a few days earlier, she said), and every once in a while the cart would slip out of her hands and go bounding down the street. At one point someone nearly snatched it away from her. After that, I decided to keep one hand on her cart and one hand on my own, and that slowed down our progress even more. We traveled along the edges of the sixth census zone, veering away from the clusters of toll mounds on Memory Avenue, and then shuffled through the Office Sector on Pyramid Road where the police now have their barracks. In her rambling, disconnected way, Isabel told me quite a bit about her life. Her husband had once been a commercial sign painter, she said, but with so many businesses closing up or unable to meet costs, Ferdinand had been out of work for several years. For a while he drank too much—stealing money from Isabel's purse at night to support his sprees, or else hanging around the distillery in the fourth census zone, cadging glots from the workers by dancing for them and telling funny stories—until one day a group of men beat him up and he never went out again. Now he refused to budge, sitting in their small apartment day after day, rarely saying anything and taking no interest in their survival. Practical matters he left to Isabel, since he no longer considered such details worthy of his attention. The only thing he cared about now was his hobby: making miniature ships and putting them into bottles.

"They're so beautiful," Isabel said, "you almost want to forgive him for the way he is. Such beautiful little ships, so perfect and small. They make you want to shrink yourself down to the size of a pin, and then climb aboard and sail away...

"Ferdinand is an artist," she went on, "and even in the old days he was moody, an unpredictable sort of man. Up one minute, down the next, always something to set him off in one direction or the other. But you should have seen the signs he painted! Everyone wanted to use Ferdinand, and he did work for all kinds of shops. Drug stores, gro-

ceries, tobacconists, jewelers, taverns, book stores, everything. He had his own work place then, right in the
warehouse district downtown, a lovely little spot. But all
that's gone now: the saws, the paintbrushes, the buckets
of color, the smells of sawdust and varnish. It all got swept
away during the second purge of the eighth census zone,
and that was the end of it."

Half of what Isabel said I didn't understand. But by
reading between the lines and trying to fill in the gaps
myself, I gathered that she had had three or four children,
all of whom were either dead or had run away from home.
After Ferdinand lost his business, Isabel had become a
scavenger. You would expect a woman of her age to have
signed up as a garbage collector, but strangely enough
she chose object hunting. It struck me as the worst possible choice. She wasn't fast, she wasn't clever, and she
had no stamina. Yes, she said, she knew all that, but she
had made up for her deficiencies with certain other qualities—a curious knack of knowing where to go, an instinct
for sniffing out things in neglected places, an inner magnet
that somehow seemed to draw her to the right spot. She
couldn't explain it herself, but the fact was that she had
made some startling finds: a whole bag of lace underwear
that she and Ferdinand had been able to live off of for
almost a month, a perfectly intact saxophone, a sealed
carton of brand-new leather belts (straight from the fac-
tory it seemed, although the last belt manufacturer had
been out of business for more than five years), and an
Old Testament printed on rice paper with calfskin binding
and gilt-edged pages. But that was some time ago, she
said, and for the past six months she had been losing her
touch. She was worn out, too tired to stay on her feet for

very long, and her mind now wandered constantly from her work. Nearly every day she would discover herself walking down a street she did not recognize, turning a corner without knowing where she had just been, entering a neighborhood and thinking she was somewhere else. "It was a miracle that you happened to be there," she said, as we paused to rest in a doorway. "But it wasn't an accident. I have prayed to God for so long now that he finally sent someone to rescue me. I know that people don't talk about God anymore, but I can't help myself. I think about him every day, I pray to him at night when Ferdinand is asleep, I talk to him in my heart all the time. Now that Ferdinand won't say anything to me anymore, God is my only friend, the only one who listens to me. I know he is very busy and doesn't have time for an old woman like me, but God is a gentleman, and he has me on his list. Today, at long last, he paid me a visit. He sent you to me as a sign of his love. You are the dear, sweet child that God has sent to me, and now I am going to take care of you, I am going to do everything I can for you. No more sleeping outside, no more roaming the streets from morning to night, no more bad dreams. All that's over now, I promise you. As long as I'm alive, you'll have a place to live, and I don't care what Ferdinand says. From now on, there will be a roof over your head and food to eat. That's how I'm going to thank God for what he has done. He has answered my prayers, and now you are my dear, sweet, little child, my darling Anna who came to me from God."

Their house was on Circus Lane, deep inside a network of small alleys and dirt paths that wound through the heart

of the second census zone. This was the oldest section of
the city, and I had been there only once or twice before.
Pickings for scavengers were slim in this neighborhood,
and I had always been nervous about getting lost in its
mazelike streets. Most of the houses were made of wood,
and this made for a number of curious effects. Instead of
eroding bricks and crumbling stones, with their jagged
heaps and dusty residues, things here seemed to lean and
sag, to buckle under their own weight, to be twisting themselves slowly into the ground. If the other buildings were
somehow flaking to bits, these buildings were withering,
like old men who had lost their strength, arthritics who
could no longer stand up. Many of the roofs had caved in,
shingles had rotted away to the texture of sponge, and here
and there you could see entire houses leaning in two opposite directions, standing precariously like giant paral-
lelograms—so nearly on their last legs that one touch of
the finger, one tiny breath, would send them crashing to
the ground.

The building that Isabel lived in was made of brick,
however. There were six floors with four small apartments
on each, a dark staircase with worn, wobbling steps, and
peeling paint on the walls. Ants and cockroaches moved
about unmolested, and the whole place stank of turned
food, unwashed clothes, and dust. But the building itself
seemed reasonably solid, and I could only think of how
lucky I was. Note how quickly things change for us. If
someone had told me before I came here that this was
where I would wind up living, I would not have believed
it. But now I felt blessed, as though some great gift had
been bestowed on me. Squalor and comfort are relative
terms, after all. Just three or four months after coming to

the city, I was willing to accept this new home of mine without the slightest shudder.

Ferdinand did not make much noise when Isabel announced that I would be moving in with them. Tactically, I think she went about it in the right way. She did not ask his permission for me to stay there, she simply informed him that there were three people in the household now instead of two. Since Ferdinand had relinquished all practical decisions to his wife long ago, it would have been difficult for him to assert his authority in this one area without tacitly conceding that he should assume more responsibility in others. Nor did Isabel bring the question of God into it, as she had done with me. She gave a deadpan account of the facts, telling him how I had saved her, adding the where and the when, but with no flourishes or commentary. Ferdinand listened to her in silence, pretending not to pay attention, shooting a furtive glance at me every now and then, but mostly just staring off toward the window, acting as though none of this concerned him. When Isabel had finished, he seemed to consider it for a moment, then shrugged. He looked at me directly for the first time and said, "It's too bad you went to all that trouble. The old bone bag would be better off dead." Then, without waiting for me to answer, he withdrew to his chair in the corner of the room and went back to work on his tiny model ship.

Ferdinand was not as bad as I thought he would be, however, at least not in the beginning. An uncooperative presence, to be sure, but with none of the outright malice I was expecting. His fits of bad temper came in short, fractious bursts, but most of the time he said nothing, stubbornly refusing to talk to anyone, brooding in his corner like some

51

aberrant creature of ill will. Ferdinand was an ugly man, and there was nothing about him that made you forget his ugliness—no charm, no generosity, no redeeming grace. He was bone-thin and hunched, with a large hook nose and a half-bald head. The little hair he had left was frizzy and unkempt, sticking out furiously on all sides, and his skin had a sick man's pallor—an unearthly white, made to seem even whiter because of the black hair that grew all over him—on his arms, his legs, and chest. Perpetually unshaven, dressed in rags, and never once with a pair of shoes on his feet, he looked like someone's cartoon version of a beachcomber. It was almost as though his obsession with ships had led him to play out the role of a man marooned on a desert island. Or else it was the opposite. Already stranded, perhaps he had begun building ships as a sign of inner distress—as a secret call for rescue. But that did not mean he thought the call would be answered. Ferdinand was never going anywhere again, and he knew it. In one of his more affable moods, he once confessed to me that he had not set foot outside the apartment in over four years. "It's all death out there," he said, gesturing toward the window. "There are sharks in those waters, and whales that can swallow you whole. Hug to the shore is my advice, hug to the shore and send up as many smoke signals as you can."

Isabel had not exaggerated Ferdinand's talents, however. His ships were remarkable little pieces of engineering, stunningly crafted, ingeniously designed and put together, and as long as he was furnished with enough materials—scraps of wood and paper, glue, string, and an occasional bottle— he was too absorbed by his work to stir up much trouble in the house. I learned that the best way to get along with him was to pretend he wasn't there. In the beginning, I went out of my way to prove my peaceful intentions, but Ferdinand was so embattled, so thoroughly disgusted with himself and the world, that no good came of it. Kind words meant nothing to him, and more often than not he would turn them into threats. Once, for example, I made the mistake of admiring his ships out loud and suggesting that they would fetch a lot of money if he ever chose to sell them. But Ferdinand was outraged. He jumped up from his chair and started lurching around the room, waving his penknife in my face. "Sell my fleet!" he shouted. "Are you crazy? You'll have to kill me first. I won't part with a single one—not ever! It's a mutiny, that's what it is. An insurrection! One more word out of you, and you'll walk the plank!"

His only other passion seemed to be catching the mice that lived in the walls of the house. We could hear them scampering around in there at night, gnawing away at whatever minuscule pickings they had found. The racket got so loud at times that it disrupted our sleep, but these were clever mice and not readily prone to capture. Ferdinand rigged up a small trap with wire mesh and wood, and each night he would dutifully set it with a piece of bait. The trap did not kill the mice. When they wandered in for the food, the door would shut behind them, and they would be locked inside the cage. This happened only once or twice a month, but on those mornings when Ferdinand woke up and discovered a mouse in there, he nearly went mad with happiness—hopping around the cage and clapping his hands, snorting boisterously in an adenoidal rush of laughter. He would pick up the mouse by the tail, and then, very methodically, roast it over the flames of the stove. It was a terrible thing to watch, with the mouse wriggling and squeaking for dear life, but Ferdinand would

53

just stand there, entirely engrossed in what he was doing, mumbling and cackling to himself about the joys of meat. A breakfast banquet for the captain, he would announce when the singeing was done, and then, chomp, chomp, slobbering with a demonic grin on his face, devour the creature fur and all, carefully spitting out the bones as he chewed. He would put the bones on the window sill to dry, and eventually they would be used as pieces for one of his ships—as masts or flagpoles or harpoons. Once, I remember, he took apart a set of mouse's ribs and used them as oars for a galley ship. Another time, he used a mouse's skull as a figurehead and attached it to the prow of a pirate schooner. It was a bright little piece of work, I have to admit, even if it disgusted me to look at it.

On days when the weather was good, Ferdinand would position his chair in front of the open window, lay his pillow on the sill, and sit there for hours on end, crouched forward, his chin in his hands, looking out at the street below. It was impossible to know what he was thinking, since he never uttered a word, but every now and then, say an hour or two after one of these vigils had ended, he would begin babbling in a ferocious voice, spewing out streams of belligerent nonsense. "Grind 'em all up," he would blurt out. "Grind 'em up and scatter the dust. Pigs, every last one of them! Wobble me down, my fine-feathered foe, you'll never get me here. Huff and puff, I'm safe where I am." One non sequitur after another, rushing out of him like some poison that had accumulated in his blood. He would rant and rave like this for fifteen or twenty minutes, and then, abruptly, without any warning at all, he would fall silent again, as though the storm inside him had suddenly been calmed.

During the months I lived there, Ferdinand's ships gradually became smaller and smaller. From whiskey bottles and beer bottles, he worked his way down to bottles of cough syrup and test tubes, then down to empty vials of perfume, until at last he was constructing ships of almost microscopic proportions. The labor was inconceivable to me, and yet Ferdinand never seemed to tire of it. And the smaller the ship, the more attached to it he became. Once or twice, waking up in the morning a little earlier than usual, I actually saw Ferdinand sitting by the window and holding a ship in the air, playing with it like a six-year-old, whooshing it around, steering it through an imaginary ocean, and muttering to himself in several voices, as though acting out the parts in a game he had invented. Poor, stupid Ferdinand. "The smaller the better," he said to me one night, bragging about his accomplishments as an artist. "Some day I'll make a ship so small that no one can see it. Then you'll know who you're dealing with, my smart-ass little tramp. A ship so small that no one can see it! They'll write a book about me, I'll be so famous. Then you'll see what's what, my vicious little slut. You'll never know what hit you. Ha, ha! you won't even have a clue!"

We lived in one medium-sized room, about fifteen feet by twenty. There was a sink, a small camp stove, a table, two chairs—later a third—and a chamber pot in one corner, separated from the rest of the room by a flimsy sheet. Ferdinand and Isabel slept apart, each in a different corner, and I slept in a third. There were no beds, but with a blanket folded under me to cushion the floor, I was not uncomfortable. Compared to the months I had spent in the open, I was very comfortable.

My presence made things easier for Isabel, and for a time she seemed to regain some of her strength. She had been doing all the work herself—object hunting in the streets, trips to the Resurrection Agents, buying food at the municipal market, cooking dinner at home, emptying the slops in the morning—and at least now there was someone to share the burden with her. For the first few weeks, we did everything together. Looking back on it now, I would say those were the best days we had: the two of us out in the street before the sun was up, roaming through the quiet dawns, the deserted alleyways, the broad boulevards all around. It was spring then, the latter part of April, I think, and the weather was deceptively good, so good that you felt it would never rain again, that the cold and the wind had vanished forever. We would take only one cart with us, leaving the other one back at the house, and I would push it along slowly, moving at Isabel's pace, waiting for her to get her bearings, to size up the prospects around us. Everything she had said about herself was true. She had an extraordinary talent for this kind of work, and even in her weakened state she was as good as anyone I had ever watched. At times I felt she was a demon, an out and out witch who found things by magic. I kept asking her to explain how she did it, but she was never able to say much. She would pause, think seriously for several moments, and then make some general comment about sticking to it or not giving up hope—in terms so vague that they were of no help to me at all. Whatever I finally learned from her came from watching, not listening, and I absorbed it by a kind of osmosis, in the same way you learn a new language. We would take off blindly, wandering more or less at random until Isabel had an intuition about where we should look, and then I would go trotting off to the spot, leaving her behind to protect the cart. Considering the shortages in the streets at the time, our hauls were quite good, enough to keep us going in any case, and there was no question that we worked well together. We didn't do much talking in the streets, however. That was a danger Isabel warned me against many times. Never think about anything, she said. Just melt into the street and pretend your body doesn't exist. No musings; no sadness or happiness; no anything but the street, all empty inside, concentrating only on the next step you are about to take. Of all the advice she gave me, it was the one thing I ever understood.

Even with my help, however, and the many fewer miles she had to walk every day, Isabel's strength began to fail her. Bit by bit, it came harder for her to manage the outdoors, to negotiate the long hours spent on her feet, and one morning, inevitably, she just couldn't get up anymore, the pains in her legs were so bad, and I went out alone. And from that day on, I did all the work myself.

These are the facts, and one by one I am telling them to you. I took over the day-to-day affairs of the household. I was the one in charge, the one who did everything. I'm sure that will make you laugh. You remember how it used to be for me at home: the cook, the maid, the clean laundry folded and put in my bureau drawers every Friday. I never had to lift a finger. The whole world was given to me, and I never even questioned it: piano lessons, art lessons, summers by the lake in the country, trips abroad with my friends. Now I had become a drudge, the sole support of two people I would never even have met in my old life. Isabel, with her lunatic purity and goodness; Ferdinand, adrift in his coarse, demented angers. It was all so strange, so improbable. But the fact was that Isabel had saved my life just as surely as I had saved hers, and it never occurred to me not to do what I could. From being a little waif they dragged in off the street, I became the exact measure that stood between them and total ruin. Without me, they would not have lasted ten days. I don't mean to boast about what I did, but for the first time in my life there were people who depended on me, and I did not let them down.

In the beginning, Isabel kept insisting that she was all right, that nothing was wrong with her that a few days' rest couldn't cure. "I'll be back on my feet before you know it," she would say to me as I left in the morning. "It's just a temporary problem." But that illusion was soon toppled. Weeks went by, and her condition did not change. By midspring it became clear to both of us that she wasn't going to get any better. The worst blow came when I had to sell her shopping cart and scavenger's license to a black market dealer in the fourth census zone. That was the ultimate acknowledgment of her illness, but there was nothing else we could do. The cart was just sitting in the house day after day, of no use to anyone, and we badly needed the money at the time. True to form, it was Isabel herself who finally suggested that I go ahead and do it, but that didn't mean it wasn't hard for her.

After that, our relationship changed somewhat. We were no longer equal partners, and because she felt so guilty about saddling me with extra work, she became extremely protective of me, almost hysterical on the subject of my welfare. Not long after I began doing the scavenging by myself, she launched a campaign to change my appearance. I was too pretty for daily contact with the streets, she said, and something had to be done about it. "I just can't bear to see you go off like that every morning," she explained. "Terrible things are happening to young girls all the time, such terrible things I can't even talk about them. Oh, Anna, my dear little child, if I lost you now, I'd never forgive myself, I'd die on the spot. There's no place for vanity anymore, my angel—you have to give all that up." Isabel spoke with such conviction that she started to cry, and I understood that it would be better to go along with her than put up an argument. To tell the truth, I was very upset. But I had already seen some of those things she couldn't talk about, and there wasn't much I could say to contradict her. The first thing to go was my hair—and that was an awful business. It was all I could do not to burst into tears, and with Isabel snipping away at me, telling me to be brave, and yet all the while trembling herself, on the verge of blubbering some dark maternal sadness, it only made things worse. Ferdinand was there, too, of course, sitting in his corner, arms folded across his chest, watching the scene with cruel detachment. He laughed as my hair fell to the ground, and as it continued to fall he said that I was beginning to look like a dyke, and wasn't it funny that Isabel should be doing this to me, now that her cunt was all dried up like a piece of wood. "Don't listen to him, my angel," Isabel kept saying into my ear, "don't pay any attention to what that ogre says." But it was hard not to listen to him, hard not to be affected by that malicious laugh of his. When Isabel was finally done, she handed me a small mirror and told me to take a look. The first few moments were frightening. I looked so ugly that I didn't recognize myself anymore. It was as though I had been

59

turned into someone else. What's happened to me? I thought. Where am I? Then, at just that moment, Ferdinand broke out laughing again, a real bellyful of spite, and that was too much for me. I flung the mirror across the room and nearly hit him in the face with it. It flew past his shoulder, smacked against the wall, and clattered to the floor in fragments. For a moment or two Ferdinand just gaped, not quite believing I had done it, and then he turned to Isabel, all shaking with anger, totally beside himself, and said, "Did you see that? She tried to kill me! The fucking bitch tried to kill me!" But Isabel was not about to sympathize with him, and a few minutes later he finally shut up. From then on, he never said another word about it, did not mention the subject of my hair again.

Eventually, I learned to live with it. It was the idea of the thing that bothered me, but when you got right down to it, I don't think I looked too bad. Isabel wasn't intending to make me look like a boy, after all—no disguises, no false moustaches—but only to make the feminine things about me less apparent, my protruberances, as she called them. I was never much of a tomboy anyway, and pretending to be one now wouldn't have worked. You remember my lipsticks and outrageous earrings, my tight skirts and skimpy hems. I always loved to dress up and play the vamp, even when we were kids. What Isabel wanted was for me to call as little attention to myself as possible, to make sure that heads did not turn when I walked by. So, after my hair was gone, she gave me a cap, a loose-fitting jacket, woolen trousers, and a pair of sensible shoes—which she had bought only recently for herself. The shoes were a size too big, but an extra pair of socks seemed to eliminate the problem of blisters. With my body now enveloped in this outfit, my breasts and hips were fairly well hidden, which left precious little for anyone to lust after. It would have taken a strong imagination to see what was really there, and if anything is in short supply in the city, it's imagination.

That was how I lived. Up early in the morning and out, the long days in the streets, and then home again at night. I was too busy to think about much of anything, too exhausted to step back from myself and look ahead, and each night after supper I only wanted to collapse in my corner and go to sleep. Unfortunately, the incident with the mirror had caused a change in Ferdinand, and a tension grew up between us that became nearly intolerable. Coupled with the fact that he now had to spend his days at home with Isabel—which deprived him of his freedom and solitude— I became the focus of his attention whenever I was around. I am not just talking about his grumbling, nor the constant little digs he would make about how much money I earned or the food I brought home for our meals. No, all that was to be expected from him. The problem was more pernicious than that, more devastating in the fury that lay behind it. I had suddenly become Ferdinand's only relief, his only avenue of escape from Isabel, and because he despised me, because my very presence was a torment to him, he went out of his way to make things as difficult for me as possible. He literally sabotaged my life, pestering me at every opportunity, assailing me with a thousand tiny attacks I had no way of warding off. Early on, I had a sense of where it was all going to lead, but nothing had ever prepared me for this kind of thing, and I didn't know how to defend myself.

You know all about me. You know what my body needs and does not, what squalls and hungers lurk inside it. Those things do not disappear, even in a place like this. Granted, there are fewer opportunities to indulge your thoughts here, and when you walk through the streets you must gird yourself to the quick, purging your mind of all erotic digressions—but still, there are moments when you are alone, in bed at night for example, with the world all dark around you, and it becomes hard not to imagine yourself in various situations. I won't deny how lonely I felt in my corner. Things like that can drive you crazy sometimes. There is an ache inside you, a horrendous, clamoring ache, and unless you do something about it, there will never be an end to it. God knows that I tried to control myself, but there were times when I couldn't stand it anymore, times when I thought my heart would explode. I would shut my eyes and tell myself to go to sleep, but my brain would be in such turmoil, heaving up images of the day I had just spent, taunting me with a pandemonium of streets and bodies, and with Ferdinand's insults still fresh in my mind to add to the chaos, sleep simply would not come. The only thing that seemed to have any effect was to masturbate. Forgive me for being so blunt, but I don't see any point in mincing words. It's a common enough solution for all of us, and under the circumstances, I didn't have much choice. Almost without being aware of it, I would begin to touch my body, pretending that my hands belonged to someone else— rubbing my palms lightly over my stomach, stroking the insides of my thighs, sometimes even grabbing hold of my buttocks and working away at the flesh with my fingers, as if there were two of me and we were in each other's arms. I understood that this was only a sad little game, but my body would nevertheless respond to these tricks, and eventually I would feel an ooze of wetness gathering below. The middle finger of my right hand would do the rest, and once it was over, a languor would crawl into my bones, weighing down my eyelids until I finally sank into sleep.

All well and good, perhaps. The problem was that in such cramped quarters it was dangerous to make even the slightest sound, and on certain nights I must have slipped, must have allowed a sigh or whimper to escape from me at the crucial moment. I say this because I soon learned that Ferdinand had been listening to me, and with a sordid mind like his, it did not take long for him to figure out what I was up to. Little by little, his insults became more sexual in tone—a barrage of insinuations and ugly cracks. One minute he would call me a dirty-minded little whore, the next minute he would say that no man would ever want to touch a frigid beast like me—each statement contradicting the others, coming at me from all sides, never letting up. It was a squalid story from top to bottom, and I knew it would end badly for all of us. A seed had been lodged in Ferdinand's brain, and there was no way to get it out. He was mustering his courage, gearing up to take action, and each day I could see him becoming bolder, more sure of himself, more committed to his plan. I had had that bad experience with the Tollist on Muldoon Boulevard, but that was out in the open, and I had been able to run away from him. This was a different story. The apartment was too small, and if anything happened there, I would be trapped. Short of never going to sleep again, I had no idea what to do.

It was summer, which month I forget. I remember the heat, the long days boiling in the blood, the airless nights. The sun would go down, but the torrid air still hung over you, thick with its unbreathable smells. It was on one of those nights that Ferdinand finally made his move—inching across the room on all fours, coming toward my bed with dim-witted stealth. For reasons I still do not understand, all my panic subsided the moment he touched me. I had been lying there in the darkness, pretending to be asleep, not knowing whether I should try to fight him off or just scream as loudly as I could. Now, it suddenly became clear to me that I should do neither one of those things. Ferdinand placed his hand on my breast and let out a snickering little laugh, one of those smug, abject noises that can only come from people who are in fact already dead, and at that moment I knew precisely what I was going to do. There was a depth of certainty to this knowledge that I had never felt before. I did not struggle, I did not cry out, I did not react with any part of myself that I could recognize as my own. Nothing seemed to matter anymore. I mean nothing at all. There was this certainty inside me, and it destroyed everything else. The moment Ferdinand touched me, I knew that I was going to kill him, and the certainty was so great, so overpowering, that I almost wanted to stop and tell him about it, just so he would be able to understand what I thought of him and why he deserved to be dead.

He slid his body closer to mine, stretching out along the edge of the pallet, and began to nuzzle his rough face against my neck, muttering to me about how he had been right all along, and yes, he was going to fuck me, and yes, I was going to love every second of it. His breath smelled of the beef jerky and turnips we had eaten for dinner, and we were both sweating bullets, our bodies totally covered with sweat. The air was suffocating in that room, utterly without movement, and each time he touched me I could feel the salt water slide across my skin. I did nothing to stop him, just lay there limp and passionless without saying a word. After a while, he began to forget himself, I could feel it, could feel him foraging around my body, and then, when he started to climb on top of me, I put my fingers around his neck. I did it lightly at first, pretending to be playing with him, as though I had finally succumbed to his charms, his irresistible charms, and because of that he suspected nothing. Then I began to squeeze, and a sharp little gagging sound came out of his throat. In that first instant after I began to apply the pressure, I felt an immense happiness, a surging, uncontrollable sense of rapture. It was as though I had crossed some inner threshold, and all at once the world became different, a place of unimaginable simplicity. I shut my eyes, and then it began to feel as if I were flying through empty space, moving through an enormous night of blackness and stars. As long as I held on to Ferdinand's throat, I was free. I was beyond the pull of the earth, beyond the night, beyond any thought of myself.

Then came the oddest part of it. Just when it became clear to me that a few more moments of pressure would finish the job, I let go. It had nothing to do with weakness, nothing to do with pity. My grip around Ferdinand's throat was like iron, and no amount of thrashing and kicking would ever have loosened it. What happened was that I suddenly became aware of the pleasure I was feeling. I don't know how else to describe it, but right there at the end, as I lay on my back in the sweltering darkness, slowly squeezing the life out of Ferdinand, I understood that I was not killing him in self-defense—I was killing him for the pure pleasure of it. Horrible consciousness, horrible, horrible consciousness. I let go of Ferdinand's throat and pushed him away from me as violently as I could. I felt nothing but disgust, nothing but outrage and bitterness. It almost didn't matter that I had stopped. A few seconds either way was all it meant, but now I understood that I was no better than Ferdinand, no better than anyone else.

A tremendous, wheezing gasp emerged from Ferdinand's lungs, a miserable, inhuman sound like the braying of a donkey. He writhed around on the floor and clutched his throat, chest heaving in panic, desperately gulping air, sputtering, coughing, retching up the catastrophe all over himself. "Now you understand," I said to him. "Now you know what you're up against. The next time you try something like that, I won't be so generous."

I didn't even wait until he had fully recovered. He was going to live, and that was enough, that was more than enough. I scrambled into my clothes and left the apartment, walking down the stairs and out into the night. It had all happened so quickly. From beginning to end, I realized, the whole thing had taken just a few minutes. And Isabel had slept through it. That was a miracle in itself. I had come within an inch of killing her husband, and Isabel had not even stirred in her bed.

I wandered aimlessly for two or three hours, then returned to the apartment. It was getting on toward 4:00 A.M., and Ferdinand and Isabel were both asleep in their usual corners. I figured I had until six before the craziness began: Ferdinand storming about the room, flapping his arms, frothing at the mouth, accusing me of one crime after another. There was no way that wasn't going to happen. My

66

only uncertainty was how Isabel would react to it. Instinct told me she would take my side, but I couldn't be sure. One never knows what loyalties will surface at the critical moment, what conflicts can be churned up when you least expect them. I tried to prepare myself for the worst—knowing that if things went against me, I would be out on the street again that very day.

Isabel woke first, as she usually did. It was not an easy business for her, since the pains in her legs were generally sharpest in the morning, and it often took twenty or thirty minutes before she found the courage to stand up. That morning was particularly grueling for her, and as she slowly went about the job of gathering herself together, I puttered around the apartment as I usually did, trying to act as though nothing had happened: boiling water, slicing bread, setting the table—just sticking to the normal routine. On most mornings, Ferdinand went on sleeping until the last possible moment, rarely budging until he could smell the porridge cooking on the stove, and neither one of us paid any attention to him now. His face was turned toward the wall, and to all appearances he was simply clinging to sleep a little more stubbornly than usual. Considering what he had been through the night before, that seemed logical enough, and I didn't give it a second thought.

Eventually, however, his silence became conspicuous. Isabel and I had both completed our various preparations and were ready to sit down to breakfast. Ordinarily, one of us would have roused Ferdinand by then, but on this morning of mornings neither one of us said a word. A curious kind of reluctance seemed to hover in the air, and after a while I began to sense that we were avoiding the subject on purpose, that each of us had decided to let the other speak first. I had my own reasons for keeping quiet, of course, but Isabel's behavior was unprecedented. There was an eeriness at the core of it, a hint of defiance and jangled nerves, as though some imperceptible shift had taken place in her. I didn't know what to make of it. Perhaps I had been wrong about last night, I thought. Perhaps she had been awake; perhaps her eyes had been open, and she had seen the whole nasty business.

"Are you all right, Isabel?" I asked.

"Yes, my dear. Of course I'm all right," she said, giving me one of her dotty, cherubic smiles.

"Don't you think we should wake up Ferdinand? You know how he gets when we start without him. We don't want him to think we're cheating him out of his share."

"No, I don't suppose we do," she said, letting out a small sigh. "It's just that I was enjoying this moment of companionship. We so rarely get to be alone anymore. There's something magical about a silent house, don't you think?"

"Yes, Isabel, I do. But I also think it's time to wake up Ferdinand."

"If you insist. I was only trying to delay the moment of reckoning. Life can be so wonderful, after all, even in times like these. It's a pity that some people think only of spoiling it."

I said nothing in response to these cryptic remarks. Something was obviously not right, and I was beginning to suspect what it was. I walked over to Ferdinand's corner, crouched down beside him, and put my hand on his shoulder. Nothing happened. I gave the shoulder a shake, and when Ferdinand still didn't move, I rolled him over on his back. For the first instant or two, I didn't see anything at all. There was only a sensation, an urgent tumult of sensation that came rushing through me. This is a dead man, I said to myself. Ferdinand is a dead man, and I am looking at him with my own two eyes. It was only then, after I had spoken these words to myself, that I actually saw the condition of his face: his eyes bulging in their sockets, his tongue sticking out of his mouth, the dried blood clotted around his nose. It was not possible that Ferdinand should be dead, I thought. He had been alive when I left the apartment, and there was no way my hands could have done this. I tried to close his mouth, but his jaws were already stiff, and I couldn't move them. It would have meant breaking the bones in his face, and I didn't have the strength for it.

"Isabel," I said in a quiet voice. "I think you'd better come over here."

"Is something wrong?" she asked. Her voice betrayed nothing, and I couldn't tell if she knew what I was going to show her or not.

"Just come here and see for yourself."

As she had been forced to do of late, Isabel shuffled across the room holding on to her chair for support. When she reached Ferdinand's corner, she maneuvered herself back into the chair, paused to catch her breath, and then looked down at the corpse. For several moments she just stared at it, utterly detached, showing no emotion whatsoever. Then, very suddenly, without the smallest gesture or noise, she began to cry—almost unconsciously, it seemed, the tears just pouring out of her eyes and falling down her cheeks. It was the way young children sometimes cry—without any sobbing or shortness of breath: water flowing evenly from two identical spigots.

"I don't think Ferdinand is ever going to wake up again,"

69

she said, still looking down at the body. It was as though she could not look anywhere else, as though her eyes would be fixed on that spot forever.

"What do you think happened?"

"Only God knows that, my dear. I wouldn't even presume to guess."

"He must have died in his sleep."

"Yes, I suppose that makes sense. He must have died in his sleep."

"How do you feel, Isabel?"

"I don't know. It's too early to tell. But right now I think I'm happy. I know it's a terrible thing to say, but I think I'm very happy."

"It's not terrible. You deserve a little peace as much as anyone else."

"No, my dear, it's terrible. But I can't help it. I hope God will forgive me. I hope he will find it in his heart not to punish me for the things I am feeling now."

Isabel spent the rest of the morning fussing over Ferdinand's body. She refused to let me help, and for several hours I just sat in my corner and watched her. It was pointless to put any clothes on Ferdinand, of course, but Isabel would not have it any other way. She wanted him to look like the man he had been years ago, before anger and self-pity had destroyed him.

She washed him with soap and water, shaved off his beard, trimmed his nails, and then dressed him in the blue suit that he had worn on special occasions in the past. For several years she had kept this suit hidden under a loose floorboard, afraid that Ferdinand would bully her into selling it if he ever found out where it was. The suit was too big for him now, and she had to make a new notch in his belt to secure the pants around his waist. Isabel worked with incredible slowness, laboring over each detail with maddening precision, never once pausing, never once speeding up, and after a while it began to get on my nerves. I wanted everything to be done with as quickly as possible, but Isabel paid no attention to me. She was so wrapped up in what she was doing, I doubt that she even knew I was there. As she worked, she kept talking to Ferdinand, scolding him in a soft voice, rattling on as though he could hear her, as though he were listening to every word she said. With his face still locked in that horrible death-grimace, I don't suppose he had much choice but to let her speak. It was her last chance, after all, and for once there was nothing he could do to stop her.

She dragged it out until the end of the morning—combing his hair, brushing lint from his jacket, arranging and rearranging him as though she were grooming a doll. When it was finally over, we had to decide what to do with the body. I was for carrying Ferdinand down the stairs and leaving him on the street, but Isabel felt that was too heartless. At the very least, she said, we should put him in the scavenging cart and wheel him across the city to one of the Transformation Centers. I was against that on several counts. In the first place, Ferdinand was too big, and negotiating the cart through the streets would be hazardous. I imagined the cart tipping over, saw Ferdinand falling out, saw both Ferdinand and the cart being snatched away from us by Vultures. More importantly, Isabel did not have the strength for this kind of outing, and I was worried that she would do herself some real harm. A long day spent on her feet could destroy what little remained of her health, and I wouldn't give in to her, no matter how much she cried and pleaded.

Eventually, we hit on a solution of sorts. It seemed perfectly sensible at the time, but as I look back on it now, it strikes me as bizarre. After much dithering and hesitation, we decided to drag Ferdinand up to the roof and then push him off. The idea was to make him look like a Leaper. At least the neighbors would think that Ferdinand still had some fight left in him, Isabel said. They would look up at him flying off the roof and say to themselves that this was a man who had the courage to take matters into his own hands. It wasn't hard to see how much this thought appealed to her. In our own minds, I said, we would pretend that we were throwing him overboard. That's what happens when a sailor dies at sea: he is tossed into the water by his mates. Yes, Isabel liked that very much. We would climb to the roof and pretend that we were standing on the deck of a ship. The air would be the water, and the ground would be the ocean floor. Ferdinand would have a sailor's burial, and from then on he would belong to the sea. There was something so right about this plan that it stopped all further discussion. Ferdinand would be laid to rest in Davy Jones's locker, and the sharks would finally claim him as their own.

Unfortunately, it was not as simple as it seemed. The apartment was on the top floor of the building, but there was no staircase to the roof. The only access was by way of a narrow iron ladder that led to a hatch in the ceiling—a kind of trapdoor that could be opened by pushing up from the inside. The ladder had about a dozen rungs and was no more than seven or eight feet high, but this still meant that Ferdinand had to be carried straight up with one hand, since the other hand had to hang on for balance. Isabel couldn't offer much help, and so I had to do it all myself. I tried pushing from the bottom, and then I tried pulling from the top, but I just didn't seem to have the strength for it. He was too heavy for me, too big, too awkward, and there in the stifling summer heat, with the sweat dripping into my eyes, I didn't see how it could be done. I began to wonder if we could not produce a similar effect by dragging Ferdinand back into the apartment and pushing him out the window. It would not be as dramatic, of course, but under the circumstances it seemed like a plausible alternative. Just as I was about to give up, however, Isabel had an idea. We would wrap Ferdinand in a sheet, she said, then tie another sheet to that one and use it as a rope to pull the bundle up. That was not a simple matter either, but at least I did not have to climb and carry simultaneously. I went to the roof and pulled up Ferdinand one rung at a time. With Isabel standing below, steering the bundle and making sure it did not get stuck, the body finally made it to the top. Then I lay flat on my stomach, reached my hand back down into the darkness, and helped Isabel climb up to the roof as well. I won't talk about the slips, the near disasters, the difficulties of hanging on. When she finally crawled through the trap door and inched her way over to me, we were both so exhausted that we collapsed onto the hot tar surface, unable to get up for several minutes, unable to move at all. I remember lying on my back and looking up at the sky, thinking I was about to float out of my body, struggling to catch my breath, feeling entirely crushed by the bright, insanely beating sun.

The building was not especially tall, but it was the first

time I had been so far off the ground since coming to the city. A small breeze began to stir things back and forth, and when I finally got to my feet and looked down into the jumbled world below, I was startled to discover the ocean— way out there at the edge, a strip of gray-blue light shimmering in the far distance. It was a strange thing to see the ocean like that, and I can't tell you the effect it had on me. For the first time since my arrival, I had proof that the city was not everywhere, that something existed beyond it, that there were other worlds besides this one. It was like a revelation, like a rush of oxygen into my lungs, and it almost made me dizzy to think about it. I saw one rooftop after another. I saw the smoke rising from the crematoria and the power plants. I heard an explosion from a nearby street. I saw people walking below, too small to be human anymore. I felt the wind on my face and smelled the stench in the air. Everything seemed alien to me, and as I stood there on the roof next to Isabel, still too exhausted to say anything, I suddenly felt that I was dead, as dead as Ferdinand in his blue suit, as dead as the people who were burning into smoke at the edges of the city. I became calmer than I had been in a long time, almost happy in fact, but happy in an impalpable sort of way, as though that happiness had nothing to do with me. Then, out of nowhere, I started to cry—I mean really cry, sobbing deep in my chest, my breath broken, the air all choked out of me—bawling in a way I had not done since I was a little girl. Isabel put her arms around me, and I kept my face hidden in her shoulder for a long time, sobbing my heart out for no good reason at all. I have no idea where those tears came from, but for several months after that I did not feel like myself anymore. I continued to live and breathe, to move from one place to another, but I could not escape the thought that I was dead, that nothing could ever bring me to life again.

At some point we returned to our business on the roof. It was late afternoon by then, and the heat had begun to melt the tar, dissolving it into a thick, glutinous cushion. Ferdinand's suit had not fared well during the journey up the ladder, and once we had extricated him from the sheet, Isabel went through another long bout of preparation and grooming. When the moment finally came to carry him to the edge, Isabel insisted that he should be upright. Otherwise, the purpose of the charade would be lost. We had to create the illusion that Ferdinand was a Leaper, she said, and Leapers didn't crawl, they walked boldly to the precipice with their heads held high. There was no arguing with this logic, and so we spent the next several minutes wrestling with Ferdinand's inert body, pushing and tugging at him until we got him shakily to his feet. It was a gruesome little comedy, I can tell you. The dead Ferdinand was standing between us, wobbling like some giant windup toy—hair blowing in the wind, pants sliding down his hips, and that startled, horrified expression still on his face. As we walked him toward the corner of the roof, his knees kept buckling and dragging, and by the time we got there both his shoes had fallen off. Neither one of us felt brave enough to get very close to the edge, and so we could never be sure if anyone was down in the street to see what happened. About a yard from the edge, not daring to go any further, we counted in unison to synchronize our efforts and then gave Ferdinand a hard shove, falling backward immediately so the momentum would not carry us over with him. His stomach hit the edge first, which made him bounce a little, and then he toppled off. I remember listening for the sound of the body landing on the pavement, but I never heard anything but my own pulse, the sound of my heart beating in my head. That was the last we ever saw of Ferdinand. Neither one of us went down to the street for the rest of the day, and when I went out the next morning to begin my rounds with the cart, Ferdinand was gone, along with everything he had been wearing.

I stayed with Isabel until the end. That includes the summer and the fall, and then a little bit beyond—to the edge of winter, just as the cold began to strike in earnest. In all those months we never talked about Ferdinand—not about his life, not about his death, not about anything. I found it hard to believe that Isabel had mustered the strength or the courage to kill him, but that was the only explanation that made sense to me. There were many times when I was tempted to ask her about that night, but I could never bring myself to do it. It was Isabel's business somehow, and unless she wanted to talk about it, I did not feel I had the right to question her.

This much was certain: neither one of us was sorry that he was gone. A day or two after the ceremony on the roof, I gathered up all his possessions and sold them, right down to the model ships and a half-empty tube of glue, and Isabel did not say a word. It should have been a time of new possibilities for her, but things did not work out that way. Her health continued to deteriorate, and she was never really able to take advantage of life without Ferdinand. In fact, after that day on the roof, she never left the apartment again.

I knew that Isabel was dying, but I did not think it would happen so fast. It began with her not being able to walk anymore, and then, little by little, the weakness spread, until it was no longer just her legs that wouldn't work, but everything, from her arms down into her spine, and finally even her throat and mouth. It was a kind of sclerosis, she told me, and there was no cure for it. Her grandmother had died of the same disease long ago, and Isabel referred to it simply as "the collapse," or "the disintegration." I could try to make her comfortable, but beyond that there was nothing to be done.

The worst part of it was that I still had to work. I still had to get myself up early in the morning and shove off through the streets, on the prowl for whatever I could find. My heart was no longer in it, and it became increasingly difficult for me to track down anything of value. I was always lagging behind myself, thoughts going in one direction, steps in another, unable to make a quick or sure move. Time and again I was beaten out by other object hunters. They seemed to swoop down from nowhere, snatching things away from me just as I was about to pick them up. This meant that I had to spend more and more time outside in order to fill my quota, all the while plagued by the thought that I should be at home taking care of Isabel. I kept imagining that something would happen to her while I was gone, that she would die without my being there, and this would be enough to throw me off completely, to make me forget the work I had to do. And believe me, this work had to be done. Otherwise, there would have been nothing for us to eat.

Toward the end, it became impossible for Isabel to move by herself. I would try to arrange her securely in bed, but because she no longer had much control over her muscles, she would inevitably start slipping again after a few minutes. These shifts of position were an agony to her, and even the weight of her own body pressing on the floor made her feel as though she were being burned alive. But pain was only part of the problem. The breakdown of muscle and bone finally reached her throat, and when that happened Isabel started losing the power of speech. A disintegrating body is one thing, but when the voice goes too, it feels as if the person is no longer there. It began with a certain sloppiness of articulation—her words slurred around the edges, the consonants getting softer and less distinct, gradually beginning to sound like vowels. I did not pay much attention to this at first. There were many more urgent things to think about, and at that point it was still possible to understand her with only a small effort. But then it continued to get worse, and I found myself straining to make sense of what she was trying to say, always managing to catch it in the end somehow, but with more and more difficulty as the days wore on. Then, one morning, I realized that she wasn't talking anymore. She was gurgling and groaning, trying to say something to me but only managing to produce an incoherent sputter, an awful noise that sounded like chaos itself. Spittle was dribbling down from the corners of her mouth, and the noise kept pouring out of her, a dirge of unimaginable confusion and pain. Isabel cried when she heard herself that morning and saw the uncomprehending look on my face, and I don't think I have ever felt sorrier for anyone than I did for her then. Bit by bit, the whole world had slipped away from her, and now there was almost nothing left.

But it was not quite the end. For about ten days, Isabel

still had enough strength to write out messages for me with a pencil. I went to a Resurrection Agent one afternoon and bought a large notebook with a blue cover. All the pages were blank, and this made it expensive, since good notebooks are extremely hard to find in the city. But it definitely seemed worth it to me, no matter what the price. The agent was a man I had done business with before—Mr. Gambino, the hunchback on China Street—and I remember haggling with him tooth and nail, the two of us going at each other for almost half an hour. I couldn't get him to lower the price of the notebook, but in the end he threw in six pencils and a little plastic sharpener at no extra cost.

Strangely enough, I am writing in that same blue notebook now. Isabel never managed to use very much of it, no more than five or six pages, and after she died I could not bring myself to throw it out. I took it along with me on my travels, and since then I have always kept it with me—the blue notebook, the six yellow pencils, and the green sharpener. If I had not found these things in my bag the other day, I don't think I would have started writing to you. But there was the notebook with all those blank pages in it, and suddenly I felt an overwhelming urge to pick up one of the pencils and begin this letter. By now it is the one thing that matters to me: to have my say at last, to get it all down on these pages before it is too late. I tremble when I think how closely everything is connected. If Isabel had not lost her voice, none of these words would exist. Because she had no more words, these other words have come out of me. I want you to remember that. If not for Isabel, there would be nothing now. I never would have begun.

In the end, what did her in was the same thing that had taken away her voice. Her throat finally stopped working altogether, and because of that she could no longer swallow. From then on, solid food was out of the question, but eventually even water became impossible for her to get down. I was reduced to putting a few drops of moisture on her lips to prevent her mouth from drying up, but we both knew that it was only a matter of time now, since she was literally starving to death, wasting away for lack of any nourishment. It was a remarkable thing, but once I even thought that Isabel was smiling at me, right there at the end, as I sat beside her dabbing water on her lips. I can't be absolutely certain, however, since she was already so far away from me by then, but I like to think that it was a smile, even if Isabel did not know what she was doing. She had been so apologetic about getting sick, so ashamed at having to rely on me for everything, but the fact was that I needed her just as much as she needed me. What happened then, right after the smile, if it was a smile, was that Isabel began to choke on her own saliva. She just couldn't get it down anymore, and though I tried to clean out her mouth with my fingers, too much of it was sliding back down her throat, and soon there was no more air left for her to breathe. The sound she made then was horrible, but it was so weak, so devoid of real struggle, that it did not last very long.

Later that same day, I gathered up a number of things from the apartment, packed them in my cart, and took them over to Progress Avenue in the eighth census zone. I wasn't thinking very clearly—I can even remember being aware of it at the time—but that didn't stand in my way. I sold dishes, clothes, bedding, pots, pans, God knows what else—anything I could get my hands on. It was a relief to be getting rid of it all, and in some way it took the place of tears for me. I couldn't cry anymore, you see, not since that day on the roof, and after Isabel died, I felt like smashing things, I felt like turning the house upside down. I took the money and went across the city to Ozone Prospect and bought the most beautiful dress I could find. It was white, with lace on the collar and sleeves, and a broad satin sash that went around the waist. I think Isabel would have been happy if she had known she was wearing it.

After that, things get a little confused for me. I was exhausted, you understand, and I had that blurring in the brain that makes you think you are no longer yourself, when you begin to drift in and out of consciousness, even though you are awake. I can remember lifting Isabel in my arms and shuddering when I felt how light she had become. It was like carrying a child, with those feathery bones and that soft, pliant body. Then I was out on the street, pushing her in the cart across the city, and I can remember being scared, feeling that everyone I passed was looking at the cart, wondering how they could attack me and steal the dress Isabel was wearing. After that, I can see myself arriving at the gate of the Third Transformation Center and waiting in line with many others—and then, when my turn came, being paid the normal fee by one of the officials. He, too, eyed Isabel's dress with more than usual interest, and I could see the wheels spinning in his sordid little head. I held up the money he had just given me and said that he could have it if he promised to burn the dress along with Isabel. Naturally he agreed—with a vulgar, complicitous wink—but I have no way of knowing if he kept his word. I tend to think not, which explains why I prefer not to think about any of this at all.

After leaving the Transformation Center, I must have wandered around for a while, my head in the clouds, paying no attention to where I was. Later, I fell asleep somewhere, probably in a doorway, but I woke up feeling no better than I had before, maybe worse. I thought about returning to the apartment, then decided that I wasn't ready to face it. I dreaded the prospect of being there alone, of going back to that room and just sitting there with nothing to do. Perhaps another few hours of fresh air would do me some good, I thought. Then, as I woke up a little more and gradually saw where I was, I discovered that I no longer had the cart. The umbilical cord was still secured around my waist, but the cart itself was gone. I looked up and down the street for it, rushing frantically from one doorway to the next, but it was no use. Either I had left it at the crematorium or it had been stolen from me while I was asleep. My mind was so fuzzed just then that I couldn't be sure which. That's all it takes. A moment or two when your attention flags, a single second when you forget to be vigilant, and then everything gets lost, all your work is suddenly wiped out. The cart was the one thing I needed to survive, and now it was gone. I couldn't have done a better job of sabotaging myself if I had taken out a razor blade and slit my throat.

That was bad enough, but the funny part was that I didn't seem to care. Objectively speaking, the loss of the cart was a disaster, but it also gave me the one thing I had been secretly wanting for a long time: an excuse to give up scavenging. I had stuck with it for Isabel's sake, but now that she was gone, I couldn't imagine myself doing it anymore. It was part of a life that had ended for me, and here was my chance to set out on a fresh course, to take my life in my own hands and do something about it.

Without even pausing in my tracks, I set out for one of the document forgers in the fifth census zone and sold my scavenger's license to him for thirteen glots. The money I earned that day would keep me going for at least two or three weeks, but now that I had started, I had no intention of stopping there. I returned to the apartment full of plans, calculating how much more money I could bring in by selling additional household articles. I worked through the night, heaping goods into a pile in the middle of the room. I ransacked the closet for every useful object, overturning boxes, riffling through drawers, and then, at about 5:00 A.M., extracted an unhoped-for bounty from Isabel's hiding place under the floor: a silver knife and fork, the gilt-edged Bible, and a little pouch stuffed with forty-eight glots in change. I spent the whole of the next day cramming the sellable items into a suitcase and tramping off to various Resurrection Agents around the city, selling one batch of things and then returning to the apartment to prepare another. All in all, I rustled up over three hundred glots (the knife and fork accounted for almost a third of that), and suddenly I had staked myself to a good five or six months in the clear. Under the circumstances, it was more than I could have asked for. I felt rich, positively on top of the world.

These high spirits did not last long, however. I went to bed that night exhausted from my selling binge, and the very next morning, less than an hour after dawn, I was awakened by a loud pounding on the door. It's strange how quickly one knows such things, but my first thought after hearing the sound of that knocking was to hope they wouldn't kill me. I did not even have a chance to stand up. The housebreakers forced the door open and then crossed the threshold with the usual bludgeons and sticks in their hands. There were three of them, and I recognized the two biggest ones as the Gunderson boys from downstairs. News must travel fast, I thought. Isabel had been dead for only two days, and already the neighbors had pounced.

"Up on the dogs, girlie," one of them said. "Time to be going now. Just move along nice and quiet, and you won't get hurt."

It was all so frustrating, so intolerable. "Give me a few minutes to pack my bag," I said, climbing out of my blankets. I did my best to be calm, to suppress my anger, knowing that any hint of violence on my part would only cause them to attack.

"Okay," said one of the others. "We'll give you three minutes. But no more than one bag. Just put your stuff in there and blow."

The miracle was that the temperature had fallen drastically during the night, and I had wound up going to bed with all my clothes on. This spared me the indignity of having to dress in front of them, but more than that—and this was finally what saved my life—I had put the three hundred glots inside my trouser pockets. I am not one to believe in clairvoyance, but it almost seems as though I knew what was going to happen in advance. The thugs eyed me closely as I filled my knapsack, but not one of them was intelligent enough to suspect where the money was hidden. Then I hustled myself out of there as fast as I could, taking the stairs two at a time. I paused briefly at the bottom to catch my breath and then pushed the front door open. The air hit me like a hammer. There was a tremendous noise of wind and cold, a rush of winter in my ears, and all around me objects were flying with crazy vehemence, crashing helter-skelter into the sides of buildings, skittering down the streets, breaking apart like so many chunks of ice. I had been in the city for more than a year now, and nothing had happened. There was some money in my pocket, but I had no job, no place to live. After all the ups and downs, I was right back where I had started.

In spite of what you would suppose, the facts are not reversible. Just because you are able to get in, that does not mean you will be able to get out. Entrances do not become exits, and there is nothing to guarantee that the door you walked through a moment ago will still be there when you turn around to look for it again. That is how it works in the city. Every time you think you know the answer to a question, you discover that the question makes no sense.

I spent several weeks trying to escape. At first, there seemed to be any number of possibilities, a whole range of methods for getting myself back home, and given the fact that I had some money to work with, I did not think it would be very hard. That was wrong, of course, but it took me a while before I was willing to admit it. I had arrived in a foreign charity ship, and it seemed logical to assume that I could return in one. I therefore made my way down to the docks, fully prepared to bribe whatever official I had to in order to book passage. No ships were in sight, however, and even the little fishing boats I had seen there a month before were gone. Instead, the whole waterfront was thronged with workers—hundreds and hundreds of them, it seemed to me, more men than I was able to count. Some were unloading rubble from trucks, others were carrying bricks and stones to the edge of the water, still others were laying the foundations for what looked like an immense sea wall or fortification. Armed police guards stood on platforms surveying the workers, and the place swarmed with din and confusion—the rumbling of engines, people running back and forth, the voices of crew chiefs shouting orders. It turned out that this was the Sea Wall Project, a public works enterprise that had recently been started by the new government. Governments come and go quite rapidly here, and it is often difficult to keep up with the changes. This was the first I had heard of the current takeover, and when I asked someone the purpose of the sea wall, he told me it was to guard against the possibility of war. The threat of foreign invasion was mounting, he said, and it was our duty as citizens to protect our homeland. Thanks to the efforts of the great So-and-So—whatever the name of the new leader was— the materials from collapsed buildings were now being collected for defense, and the project would give work to thousands of people. What kind of pay were they offering? I asked. No money, he said, but a place to live and one warm meal a day. Was I interested in signing up? No thanks, I said, I have other things to do. Well, he said, there would be plenty of time for me to change my mind. The government was estimating that it would take at least fifty years to finish the wall. Good for them, I said, but in the meantime how does one get out of here? Oh no, he said, shaking his head, that's impossible. Ships aren't allowed to come in anymore—and if nothing comes in, nothing can go out.

What about an airplane? I said. What's an airplane? he asked, smiling at me in a puzzled sort of way, as though I had just told a joke he didn't understand. An airplane, I said. A machine that flies through the air and carries people from one place to another. That's ridiculous, he said, giving me a suspicious kind of look. There's no such thing. It's impossible. Don't you remember? I asked. I don't know what you're talking about, he said. You could get into trouble for spreading that kind of nonsense. The government doesn't like it when people make up stories. It's bad for morale.

You see what you are up against here. It's not just that things vanish—but once they vanish, the memory of them vanishes as well. Dark areas form in the brain, and unless you make a constant effort to summon up the things that are gone, they will quickly be lost to you forever. I am no more immune to this disease than anyone else, and no doubt there are many such blanks inside me. A thing vanishes, and if you wait too long before thinking about it, no amount of struggle can ever wrench it back. Memory is not an act of will, after all. It is something that happens in spite of oneself, and when too much is changing all the time, the brain is bound to falter, things are bound to slip through it. Sometimes, when I find myself groping for a thought that has eluded me, I begin to drift off to the old days back home, remembering how it used to be when I was a little girl and the whole family would go up north on the train for summer holidays. Big brother William would always let me have the window seat, and more often than not I wouldn't say anything to anyone, riding with my face pressed against the window and looking out at the scenery, studying the sky and the trees and the water as the train sped through the wilderness. It was always so beautiful to me, so much more beautiful than the things in the city, and every year I would say to myself, Anna, you have never seen anything more beautiful than this—try to remember it, try to memorize all the beautiful things you are seeing, and in that way they will always be with you, even when you can't see them anymore. I don't think I ever looked harder at the world than on those train rides up north. I wanted everything to belong to me, for all that beauty to be a part of what I was, and I remember trying to remember it, trying to store it up for later, trying to hold on to it for a time when I would really need it. But the odd thing was that none of it ever stayed with me. I tried so hard, but somehow or other I always wound up losing it, and in the end the only thing I could remember was how hard I had tried. The things themselves passed too quickly, and by the time I saw them they were already flying out of my head, replaced by still more things that vanished before I could see them. The only thing that remains for me is a blur, a bright and beautiful blur. But the trees and the sky and the water—all that is gone. It was always gone, even before I had it.

It will not do, then, simply to feel disgust. Everyone is prone to forgetfulness, even under the most favorable conditions, and in a place like this, with so much actually disappearing from the physical world, you can imagine how many things are forgotten all the time. In the end, the problem is not so much that people forget, but that they do not always forget the same thing. What still exists as a memory for one person can be irretrievably lost for another, and this creates difficulties, insuperable barriers against understanding. How can you talk to someone about airplanes, for example, if that person doesn't know what an airplane is? It is a slow but ineluctable process of erasure. Words tend to last a bit longer than things, but eventually they fade too, along with the pictures they once evoked. Entire categories of objects disappear—flowerpots, for example, or cigarette filters, or rubber bands— and for a time you will be able to recognize those words, even if you cannot recall what they mean. But then, little by little, the words become only sounds, a random collection of glottals and fricatives, a storm of whirling phonemes, and finally the whole thing just collapses into gibberish. The word "flowerpot" will make no more sense to you than the word "splandigo." Your mind will hear it, but it will register as something incomprehensible, a word from a language you cannot speak. As more and more of these foreign-sounding words crop up around you, conversations become rather strenuous. In effect, each person is speaking his own private language, and as the instances of shared understanding diminish, it becomes increasingly difficult to communicate with anyone.

I had to give up the idea of going home. Of all the things that had happened to me so far, I believe that was the most difficult to take. Until then, I had deluded myself into thinking I could return whenever I wanted to. But with the sea wall now going up, with so many people mobilized to prevent departure, this comforting notion was dashed to bits. First Isabel had died, and then I had lost the apartment. My only consolation had been the thought of home, and now that suddenly had been taken from me as well. For the first time since coming to the city, I was engulfed by pessimism.

I thought about striking off in the opposite direction.

The Fiddler's Rampart stood at the western edge of the city, and a travel permit was supposedly all you needed to walk through it. Anything would be better than the city, I felt, even the unknown, but after running back and forth between several government agencies, waiting in line day after day only to be told to take my request to yet another bureau, I finally learned that the price of travel permits had risen to two hundred glots. That was out of the question, since it would mean using up the better part of my funds in one go. I heard talk of an underground organization that smuggled people out of the city for a tenth the cost, but many people were of the opinion that it was actually a ruse—a clever form of entrapment devised by the new government. Policemen were posted at the far end of the tunnel, they said, and the moment you crawled through to the other side you were arrested—and then promptly dispatched to one of the forced labor camps in the southern mining zone. I had no way of knowing whether this rumor was true or false, but finding out did not seem worth the risk. Then winter came, and the question was settled for me. Any thoughts of leaving would have to wait until spring—assuming, of course, that I was able to last until spring. Given the circumstances, nothing seemed less sure to me than that.

It was the hardest winter in memory—the Terrible Winter, as everyone called it—and even now, years after it happened, it still stands as a crucial event in the city's history, a dividing line between one period and the next.

The cold continued for five or six months. Every now and then there would be a short thaw, but these little spurts of warmth only added to the difficulties. It would snow for a week—immense, blinding storms that pummeled the city into whiteness—and then the sun would come out, burning briefly with a summer-like intensity. The snow would melt, and by mid-afternoon the streets would be flooded. The gutters would overflow with rushing water, and everywhere you looked there would be a mad sparkle of water and light, as though the whole world had been turned into a huge, dissolving crystal. Then, suddenly, the sky would grow dark, night would begin, and the temperature would fall below zero again—freezing the water so abruptly that the ice would form in weird configurations: bumps and ripples and whorls, entire waves caught in mid-undulation, a kind of geological frenzy in miniature. By morning, of course, walking would be next to impossible—people slipping all over themselves, skulls cracking on the ice, bodies flopping helplessly on the smooth, hard surfaces. Then it would snow again, and the cycle would be repeated. This went on for months, and by the time it was over, thousands and thousands were dead. For the homeless, survival was nearly out of the question, but even the sheltered and well-fed suffered innumerable losses. Old buildings collapsed under the weight of the snow, and whole families were crushed. The cold drove people out of their minds, and sitting around in an underheated apartment all day was finally not much better than being outside. People would smash up their furniture and burn it for a little warmth, and many of these fires got out of control. Buildings were destroyed almost every day, sometimes whole blocks and neighborhoods. Whenever one of these fires broke out, vast numbers of homeless people would flock to the site and stand there for as long as the building burned—revelling in the warmth, cheering the flames as they rose up into the sky. Every tree in the city was chopped down during the winter and burned for fuel. Every domestic animal disappeared; every bird was shot. Food shortages became so drastic that construction of the sea wall was suspended—just six months after it had begun—so that all available policemen could be used to guard the shipments of produce to the municipal markets. Even so, there were a number of food riots, which led to more deaths, more injuries, more disasters. No one knows how many people died during the winter, but I have heard estimates as high as one-third to one-fourth of the population.

Somehow or other, my luck held out. In late November, I came close to being arrested in a food riot on Ptolemy Boulevard. There was an endless line that day as usual, and after waiting for more than two hours in the bitter cold without advancing, three men just ahead of me began insulting a police guard. The guard pulled out his billy club and came straight toward us, ready to swing at anyone who got in his way. The policy is to hit first and ask questions later, and I knew there wouldn't be a chance for me to defend myself. Without even pausing to think, I broke out of the line and started sprinting down the street, running for all I was worth. Momentarily confused, the guard took two or three steps in my direction, but then he stopped, clearly wanting to keep his attention fixed on the crowd. If I was out of the picture, then so much the better as far as he was concerned. I kept on running, and just as I reached the corner, I heard the crowd erupt into ugly, hostile shouting behind me. This threw me into a real panic, for I knew that in a few minutes the whole area would be overwhelmed by a fresh contingent of riot police. I kept on running as fast as I could, darting down one street after another, too afraid even to look back. Finally, after a quarter of an hour, I found myself running alongside a large stone building. I couldn't tell if I was being pursued or not, but just then a door opened a few feet up ahead and I rushed right into it. A thin man with glasses and a pale face was standing on the threshold, about to step outside, and he looked at me in horror as I slipped past him. I had entered what seemed to be an office of some kind—a small room with three or four desks in it and a clutter of papers and books.

"You can't come in here," he said impatiently. "This is the library."

"I don't care if it's the governor's mansion," I said, doubling over as I tried to catch my breath. "I'm in here now, and no one's going to get me out."

"I'll have to report you," he said in a smug, prissy voice. "You can't just barge in here like that. This is the library, and no one's allowed in without a pass."

I was too flustered by his sanctimonious attitude to know what to say. I was exhausted, at the end of my rope, and instead of trying to argue with him, I just pushed him to the ground as hard as I could. It was a ridiculous thing to do, but I wasn't able to stop myself. The man's glasses went flying off his face as he hit the floor, and for a moment I was even tempted to crush them under my foot.

"Report me if you like," I said. "But I'm not leaving here until someone drags me out." Then, before he had a chance to get up, I turned around and ran through the door at the opposite end of the room.

I came into a large hall, a vast and impressive room with a high-domed ceiling and marble floors. The sudden contrast between the tiny office and this enormous space was astonishing. My footsteps echoed back to me, and it was almost as though I could hear my breath resounding against the walls. Here and there, groups of people were pacing back and forth, talking quietly among themselves, obviously absorbed in serious conversations. A number of heads turned toward me when I entered the room, but that was only a reflex, and a moment later they all turned away again. I walked past these people as calmly and discreetly as I could, looking down at the floor and pretending that I knew where I was going. After thirty or forty feet I found a staircase and began walking up.

This was the first time I had been in the National Library. It was a splendid edifice, with portraits on the walls of governors and generals, rows of Italianate columns, and beautiful inlaid marble—one of the landmark buildings of the city. As with everything else, however, its best days were behind it. A ceiling on the second floor had caved in, columns had toppled and cracked, books and papers were strewn everywhere. I continued to see clusters of people milling about—mostly men, I realized—but no one paid any attention to me. On the other side of the card catalogue shelves, I found a green leather door that led to an enclosed staircase. I followed these stairs up to the next level and then stepped out into a long, low-ceilinged hallway with numerous doors on either side of it. No one else was in the hall, and since I heard no sounds coming from behind the doors, I assumed the chambers were empty. I tried to open the first door on my right, but it was locked. The second door was also locked. Then, against all my expectations, the third door opened. Inside, five or six men were sitting around a wooden table, talking about something in urgent, animated voices. The room was bare and windowless, with yellowish paint peeling on the walls and water dripping from the ceiling. All of the men were bearded, were dressed in black clothes, and wore hats on their heads. I was so startled to discover them there that I let out a little gasp and began to shut the door. But the oldest man at the table turned and gave me a wonderful smile, a smile so filled with warmth and kindness that I hesitated.

"Is there anything we can do for you?" he asked.

His voice was heavily accented (the th's were lost, and the w had been turned into a v), but I couldn't tell which country he came from. Ist dere anyting ve can do fer yoo. Then I looked into his eyes, and a flicker of recognition shuddered through me.

"I thought all the Jews were dead," I whispered.

"There are a few of us left," he said, smiling at me again. "It's not so easy to get rid of us, you know."

"I'm Jewish, too," I blurted out. "My name is Anna Blume, and I came here from far away. I've been in the city for over a year now, looking for my brother. I don't suppose you know him. His name is William. William Blume."

"No, my dear," he said, shaking his head, "I've never met your brother." He looked over at his colleagues across the table and asked them the same question, but none of them knew who William was.

"It's been a long time," I said. "Unless he managed to escape somehow, I'm sure he's dead."

"It's very possible," the Rabbi said gently. "So many have died, you know. It's best not to expect miracles."

"I don't believe in God anymore, if that's what you mean," I said. "I gave all that up when I was a little girl."

"It's difficult not to," the Rabbi said. "When you consider the evidence, there's a good reason why so many think as you do."

"You're not going to tell me that *you* believe in God," I said.

"We talk to him. But whether or not he hears us is another matter."

"My friend Isabel believed in God," I continued. "She's dead, too. I sold her Bible for seven glots to Mr. Gambino, the Resurrection Agent. That was a terrible thing to do, wasn't it?"

"Not necessarily. There are more important things than books, after all. Food comes before prayers."

It was strange what had come over me in the presence of this man, but the more I talked to him, the more I sounded like a child. Perhaps he reminded me of how things had been when I was very young, back in the dark ages when I still believed in what fathers and teachers said to me. I can't say for sure, but the fact was that I felt on solid ground with him, and I knew that he was someone I could trust. Almost unconsciously, I found myself reaching into my coat pocket and pulling out the picture of Samuel Farr.

"I'm also looking for this man," I said. "His name is Samuel Farr, and there's a good chance that he knows what happened to my brother."

I handed the picture to the Rabbi, but after studying it for several moments, he shook his head and said that he did not recognize the face. Just as I was beginning to feel disappointed, a man at the other end of the table spoke up. He was the youngest one there, and his reddish beard was smaller and wispier than anyone else's.

"Rabbi," he said timidly. "May I say something?"

"You don't need permission, Isaac," the Rabbi said. "You can say whatever you like."

"Nothing is certain, of course, but I believe I know who that person is," the young man said. "At least, I know someone by that name. It might not be the person the young lady is looking for, but I do know the name."

"Have a look at the picture, then," the Rabbi said, sliding the photograph across the table to him.

Isaac looked, and the expression on his face was so somber, so devoid of response, that I immediately lost hope. "It's a very poor likeness," he finally said. "But now that I've had a chance to study it, I don't think there's any question that this is the man." Isaac's pale, scholarly face broke into a smile. "I've talked to him several times," he continued. "He's an intelligent man, but extremely bitter. We disagree on just about everything."

I couldn't believe what I was hearing. Before I had a chance to say a word, the Rabbi asked, "Where can this man be found, Isaac?"

"Mr. Farr is not far," Isaac said, unable to resist the pun. He giggled briefly, then added: "He lives right here in the library."

"Is it true?" I finally said. "Is it really true?"

"Of course it's true. I can take you to him right now if you like." Isaac hesitated, then turned to the Rabbi. "Assuming I have your permission."

The Rabbi looked somewhat worried, however. "Is this man attached to one of the academies?" he asked.

97

"Not that I know of," Isaac said. "I believe he's an independent. He told me that he used to work for a newspaper somewhere."

"That's right," I said. "That's exactly right. Samuel Farr is a journalist."

"And what does he do now?" the Rabbi asked, ignoring my interruption.

"He's writing a book. I don't know the subject, but I gather that it has something to do with the city. We spoke a few times in the main lobby downstairs. He asks very penetrating questions."

"Is he sympathetic?" the Rabbi asked.

"He's neutral," Isaac said, "neither for nor against. He's a tormented man, but absolutely fair, with no axes to grind."

The Rabbi turned to me to explain. "You understand that we have many enemies," he said. "Our permit is in jeopardy because we no longer have full academy status, and I have to proceed with great caution." I nodded, trying to act as though I knew what he was talking about. "But under the circumstances," he continued, "I don't see what harm it can do for Isaac to show you where this man lives."

"Thank you, Rabbi," I said. "I'm very grateful to you."

"Isaac will take you to the door, but I don't want him going any farther than that. Is that clear, Isaac?" He looked at his disciple with an air of calm authority.

"Yes, Rabbi," Isaac said.

Then the Rabbi stood up from his chair and shook my hand. "You must come back and visit me sometime, Anna," he said, suddenly looking very old, very weary. "I want to know how everything turns out."

"I'll be back," I said. "I promise."

The room was on the ninth floor, the very top of the building. Isaac scurried off the moment we got there, mumbling an inarticulate apology about not being able to stay, and then I was suddenly alone again, standing in the pitch dark hall with a tiny candle burning in my left hand. There is a law of city life that says you must never knock on a door unless you know what is on the other side. Had I come all this way only to bring down some new calamity on my head? Samuel Farr was no more than a name to me, an emblem of impossible longings and absurd hopes. I had used him as a spur to keep myself going, but now that I had finally made it to his door, I felt terrified. If the candle had not been burning down so quickly, I might never have found the courage to knock.

A harsh, unfriendly voice called out from within the room. "Go away," it said.

"I'm looking for Samuel Farr. Is that Samuel Farr in there?"

"Who wants to know?" the voice asked.

"Anna Blume," I said.

"I don't now any Anna Blume," the voice answered. "Go away."

"I'm William Blume's sister," I said. "I've been trying to find you for over a year. You can't send me away now. If you won't open the door, I'll just keep knocking until you do."

I heard a chair scrape along the floor, followed the sound of steps moving closer to me, and then heard a lock slip out of its bolt. The door opened, and suddenly I was overwhelmed with light, a huge flood of sunlight that came pouring out into the hallway from a window in the room. It took my eyes several moments to adjust. When I finally managed to make out the person in front of me, the first thing I saw was a gun—a small black pistol aimed directly at my stomach. It was Samuel Farr, all right, but he didn't look much like the photograph anymore. The robust young man in the picture had turned into a gaunt, bearded character with dark circles under his eyes, and a nervous, unpredictable energy seemed to emanate from his body. It gave him the look of someone who had not slept in a month.

"How do I know you are who you say you are?" he asked.

"Because I say it. Because you'd be stupid not to believe me."

"I need proof. I won't let you in unless you give me some proof."

"All you have to do is listen to me talk. My accent is the same as yours. We come from the same country, the same city. We probably even grew up in the same neighborhood."

"Anyone can imitate a voice. You'll have to give me more than that."

"How about this," I said, reaching into my coat pocket and pulling out the photograph.

He studied it for ten, twenty seconds, not saying a word, and gradually his whole body seemed to crumple up, to sink back into itself. By the time he looked at me again, I saw that the gun was hanging at his side.

"Good God," he said softly, almost in a whisper. "Where did you get this?"

"From Bogat. He gave it to me before I left."

"That's me," he said. "That's what I used to look like."

"I know."

"It's hard to believe, isn't it?"

"Not really. You have to remember how long you've been here."

He seemed to drift off into thought for a moment. When he looked at me again, it was as though he did not recognize me anymore.

"Who did you say you were?" He smiled apologetically, and I could see that three or four of his bottom teeth were missing.

"Anna Blume. William Blume's sister."

"Blume. As in doom and gloom, I take it."

"That's right. Blume as in womb and tomb. You have your pick."

"I suppose you want to come in, don't you?"

"Yes. That's why I'm here. We have a lot to talk about."

It was a small room, but not so small that two people could not fit into it. A mattress on the floor, a desk and chair by the window, a wood-burning stove, quantities of papers and books piled against one of the walls, clothes in a cardboard box. It reminded me of a student's dormitory room—not unlike the one you had at the university the year I came to visit you. The ceiling was low, and it slanted down toward the outer wall so sharply that you could not go to that end of the room without hunching your back. The window along that wall was extraordinary, however— a beautiful, fan-shaped object that took up almost the entire surface. It was made of thick, segmented panes of glass divided by slender lead bars, and it formed a pattern as intricate as a butterfly's wing. You could literally see for miles through the window—all the way to the Fiddler's Rampart and beyond.

Sam gestured for me to sit on the bed, then sat down in

the desk chair and swiveled it in my direction. He apologized for pointing the gun at me, but his situation was precarious, he said, and he couldn't take any chances. He had been living in the library for almost a year now, and word had got around that he had a large stash of money in his room.

"From the looks of things here," I said, "I never would have guessed you were rich."

"I don't use the money on myself. It's for the book I'm writing. I pay people to come here and talk to me. So much money per interview, depending on how long it takes. One glot for the first hour, a half glot for each additional hour. I've done hundreds of them, one story after another. I can't think of any other way to go about it. The story is so big, you understand, it's impossible for any one person to tell it."

Sam had been sent to the city by Bogat, and even now he still wondered what had possessed him to take the assignment. "We all knew that something terrible had happened to your brother," he said. "There had been no word from him for over six months, and whoever followed him there was bound to wind up in the same pot of ink. Bogat didn't let that bother him, of course. He called me into his office one morning and said, 'This is the chance you've been waiting for, young man. I'm sending you over there to replace Blume.' My instructions were clear: write the reports, find out what had happened to William, keep myself alive. Three days later, they gave me a send-off party with champagne and cigars. Bogat spoke a toast, and everyone drank to my health, shook my hand, slapped me on the back. I felt like a guest at my own funeral. But at least I didn't have three children and a tank full of goldfish waiting for me at home like Willoughby. Whatever else you might say about him, the chief is a man of feeling. I never held it against him for choosing me as the one to go. The fact was that I probably wanted to go. If not, it would have been simple enough for me to quit. So that's how it started. I packed my bags, sharpened my pencils, and said my good-byes. That was more than a year and a half ago. Needless to say, I never sent any reports, and I never found William. For the time being, it appears that I've kept myself alive. But I wouldn't want to take any bets on how long that will last."

"I was hoping you could give me something more definite about William," I said. "One way or the other."

Sam shook his head. "Nothing is definite in this place. Considering the possibilities, you should be glad of that."

"I'm not going to give up hope. Not until I know for sure."

"That's your privilege. But I don't think it would be wise to expect anything but the worst."

"That's what the Rabbi told me."

"That's what any sensible person would tell you."

Sam spoke in a jittery, self-mocking voice, skipping from one subject to another in ways that were difficult for me to follow. I had the sense of a man on the verge of collapse — of someone who had pushed himself too hard and could barely stand up anymore. He had accumulated over three thousand pages of notes, he said. If he kept working at his present pace, he felt he could finish the preliminary work on the book in another five or six months. The problem was that his money was running low, and the odds seemed to have turned against him. He couldn't afford to do the interviews anymore, and with his funds at such a dangerous ebb, he was now eating only every other day. That made things even worse, of course. The strength was being sapped out of him, and there were times when he became so dizzy that he no longer saw the words he was writing. Sometimes, he said, he would fall asleep at his desk without even knowing it.

"You'll kill yourself before you finish," I said. "And what's the point of that? You should stop writing the book and take care of yourself."

"I can't stop. The book is the only thing that keeps me going. It prevents me from thinking about myself and getting sucked up into my own life. If I ever stopped working on it, I'd be lost. I don't think I'd make it through another day."

"There's no one to read your bloody book," I said angrily. "Don't you see that? It doesn't matter how many pages you write. No one will ever see what you've done."

"You're wrong. I'm going to take the manuscript back home with me. The book will be published, and everyone will find out what's happening here."

"You don't know what you're talking about. Haven't you heard of the Sea Wall Project? It's impossible to get out of here anymore."

"I know about the Sea Wall. But that's only one place. There are others, believe me. Up along the coast to the north. Out west through the abandoned territories. When the time comes, I'll be ready."

"You won't last that long. By the time winter is over, you won't be ready for anything."

"Something will turn up. If not, well, then it won't matter to me anyway."

"How much money do you have left?"

"I don't know. Somewhere between thirty and thirty-five glots, I think."

I was flabbergasted to hear how little it was. Even if you took every possible precaution, spending only when absolutely necessary, thirty glots would not last more than three or four weeks. I suddenly understood the danger of Sam's position. He was walking straight toward his own death, and he was not even aware of it.

At that point, words started coming out of my mouth. I had no idea what they meant until I heard them myself, but by then it was too late. "I have some money," I said. "It's not so much, but it's a lot more than you have."

"Bully for you," Sam said.

"You don't understand," I said. "When I say I have money, I mean that I'd be willing to share it with you."

"Share it? What on earth for?"

"To keep us alive," I said. "I need a place to live, and you need money. If we pooled our resources, we might have a chance of making it through the winter. If not, we're both going to die. I don't think there's any question about it. We're going to die, and it's stupid to die when you don't have to."

The bluntness of my words shocked us both, and for several moments neither one of us said anything. It was all so stark, so preposterous, but somehow or other I had managed to speak the truth. My first impulse was to apologize, but as the words continued to sit in the air between us, they went on making sense, and I found myself reluctant to take them back. I believe we both understood what was happening, but that did not make it any easier to speak the next word. In similar situations, people in this city have been known to kill each other. It is almost nothing to murder someone for a room, for a pocketful of change. Perhaps what prevented us from harming each other was the simple fact that we did not belong here. We were not people of this city. We had grown up in another place, and perhaps that was enough to make us feel that we already knew something about each other. I can't say for sure. Chance had flung us together in an almost impersonal way, and that seemed to give the encounter a logic of its own, a force that did not depend on either one of us. I had made an outlandish suggestion, a wild leap into intimacy, and Sam had not said a word. The mere fact of that silence was extraordinary, I felt, and the longer it went on, the more it seemed to validate the things I had said. By the time it was over, there was nothing left to discuss.

"It's awfully cramped in here," Sam said, looking around the tiny room. "Where do you propose to sleep?"

"It doesn't matter," I said. "We'll work something out."

"William used to talk about you sometimes," he said, showing the faintest sign of a smile at the corners of his mouth. "He even warned me about you. 'Watch out for my kid sister,' he would say. 'She's a spitfire.' Is that what you are, Anna Blume, a spitfire?"

"I know what you're thinking," I said, "but you don't have to worry. I won't get in the way. I'm not stupid, after all. I know how to read and write. I know how to think. The book will get done much faster with me around."

"I'm not worried, Anna Blume. You walk in here out of the cold, plunk yourself down on my bed, and offer to make me a rich man—and you expect me to be worried?"

"You shouldn't exaggerate. It comes to less than three hundred glots. Not even two seventy-five."

"That's what I said—a rich man."

"If you say so."

"I do say so. And I also say this: it's a goddamned lucky thing for both of us the gun wasn't loaded."

That was how I survived the Terrible Winter. I lived in the library with Sam, and for the next six months that small room was the center of my world. I don't suppose it will shock you to hear that we wound up sleeping in the same bed. One would have to be made of stone to resist such a thing, and when it finally happened on the third or fourth night, we both felt foolish for having waited for so long. It was all bodies at first, a mad crush and tangle of limbs, a splurge of pent-up lust. The sense of release was enormous, and for the next few days we went at each other to the point of exhaustion. Then the pace died down, as in fact it had to, and then, little by little, over the weeks that followed, we actually fell in love. I am not just talking about tenderness or the comforts of a shared life. We fell deeply and irrevocably in love, and in the end it was as though we were married, as though we would never leave each other again.

Those were the best days for me. Not just here, you understand, but anywhere—the best days of my life. It's odd that I could have been so happy during that awful time, but living with Sam made all the difference. Outwardly, things did not change much. The same struggles still existed, the same problems still had to be confronted every day, but now I had been given the possibility of hope, and I began to believe that sooner or later our troubles were going to end. Sam knew more about the city than anyone I had ever met. He could recite the list of all the governments of the past ten years; he could give the names of governors, mayors, and countless sub-officials; he could tell the history of the Tollists, describe how the power plants were built, give detailed accounts of even the smallest sects. That he knew so much and could still feel confident about our chances of getting out—that was the thing that convinced me. Sam was not one to distort the facts. He was a journalist, after all, and he had trained himself to look skeptically at the world. No wishful thinking, no vague suppositions. If he said it was possible for us to get back home, that meant he knew it could be done.

In general, Sam was hardly optimistic, hardly what you would call an easy-going person. There was a kind of fury surging up in him all the time, and even when he slept he seemed tormented, thrashing around under the covers as though battling someone in his dreams. He was in bad shape when I moved in, malnourished, coughing constantly, and it took more than a month before he was restored to a semblance of decent health. Until then, I did nearly all the work. I went out shopping for food, I took care of emptying the slops, I cooked our meals and kept the room clean. Later on, when Sam was strong enough to brave the cold again, he began slipping out in the mornings to do the chores himself, insisting that I stay in bed to catch up on my sleep. He had a great talent for kindness, Sam did—and he loved me well, much better than I had ever expected to be loved by anyone. If his bouts of anguish sometimes cut him off from me, they were nevertheless an internal affair. The book remained his obsession, and he had a tendency to push himself too hard with it, to work beyond his threshold of tolerance. Faced with the pressure of organizing all the disparate material he had collected into something coherent, he would suddenly begin to lose faith in the project. He would call it worthless, a futile heap of papers trying to say things that could not be said, and then spin off into a depression that lasted anywhere from one to three days. These black moods were invariably followed by periods of extreme tenderness. He would buy small presents for me then—an apple, for example, or a ribbon for my hair, or a piece of chocolate. It was probably wrong of him to spend the extra money, but I found it difficult not to be moved by these gestures. I was always the practical one, the no-nonsense housewife who scrimped and fretted, but when Sam came in with some extravagance like that, I would feel overwhelmed, absolutely flooded with joy. I couldn't help it. I needed to know that he loved me, and if it meant that our money would run out a little sooner, I was willing to pay that price.

We both developed a passion for cigarettes. Tobacco is difficult to find here, and terribly expensive when you do, but Sam had made a number of black market connections while compiling the research for his book, and he was often able to find packs of twenty for as low as one or one-and-a-half glots. I am talking about real, old-fashioned cigarettes, the kind that are produced in factories and come in colorful paper wrappers with cellophane on the outside. The ones Sam bought had been stolen from the various foreign charity ships that had docked here in the past, and the brand names were usually printed in languages we could not even read. We would smoke them after it got dark, lying in bed and looking out through the big, fan-shaped window, watching the sky and its agitations, the clouds drifting across the moon, the tiny stars, the blizzards that came pouring down from above. We would blow the smoke out of our mouths and watch it float across the room, casting shadows on the far wall that dispersed the moment they formed. There was a beautiful transience in all this, a sense of fate dragging us along with it into unknown corners of oblivion. We often talked about home then, summoning up as many memories as we could, bringing back the smallest, most specific images in a kind of languorous incantation—the maple trees along Miro Avenue in October, the Roman numeral clocks in the public school classrooms, the green dragon light fixture in the Chinese restaurant across from the university. We were able to share the flavor of these things, to relive the myriad incidentals of a world we had both known since childhood, and it helped to keep our spirits up, I think, helped to make us believe that some day we would be able to return to all that.

I don't know how many people were living in the library at that time, but well over a hundred I should think, perhaps even more. The residents were all scholars and writers, remnants of the Purification Movement that had taken place during the tumult of the previous decade. According to Sam, the succeeding government had instituted a policy of tolerance, housing scholars in a number of public buildings around the city—the university gymnasium, an abandoned hospital, the National Library. These housing arrangements were fully subsidized (which explained the presence of the cast-iron stove in Sam's room and the miraculously functioning sinks and toilets on the sixth floor), and eventually the program was extended to include a number of religious groups and foreign journalists. When the next government came into power two years later, however, the policy was discontinued. Scholars were not evicted from their dwellings, but neither were they given any government support. The attrition rate was understandably high, as many scholars were forced by circumstances to go out and find other kinds of work. Those who remained had been pretty much left to their own devices, ignored by the various governments that had come in and out of power. A certain wary camaraderie had developed among the different factions in the library, at least to the extent that many of them were willing to talk to each other and exchange ideas. That explained the groups of people I had seen in the lobby on the first day. Public colloquies were held every morning for two hours—the so-called Peripatetic Hours—and everyone who lived in the library was invited to attend. Sam had met Isaac at one of these sessions, but he generally stayed away from them, finding the scholars to be without much interest except as a phenomenon in themselves—one more aspect of life in the city. Most of them were engaged in rather esoteric pursuits: hunting for parallels between current events and events in classical literature, statistical analyses of population trends, the compiling of a new dictionary, and so on. Sam had no use for these kinds of things, but he tried to stay on good terms with everyone, knowing that scholars can turn vicious when they think they are being made fun of. I got to know many of them in a casual sort of way—standing in line with my bucket at the sixth floor sink, exchanging food tips with the women, listening to the gossip—but I followed Sam's advice and did not become involved with any of them, keeping a friendly but reserved distance.

Other than Sam, the only person I talked to was the Rabbi. For the first month or so, I would visit him whenever I had a chance—a free hour in the late afternoon, for instance, or one of those rare moments when Sam was lost in his book and there were no more chores to be done. The Rabbi was often busy with his disciples, which meant that he didn't always have time for me, but we managed to get in several good talks. The thing I remember best was a comment he made to me on my last visit. I found it so startling at the time that I have continued to think about it ever since. Every Jew, he said, believes that he belongs to the last generation of Jews. We are always at the end, always standing on the brink of the last moment, and why should we expect things to be any different now? Perhaps I remember those words so well because I never saw him again after that conversation. The next time I went down to the third floor, the Rabbi was gone, and another man had taken his place in the room—a thin, bald man with wire-rimmed glasses. He was sitting at the table and writing furiously in a notebook, surrounded by piles of papers and what looked like several human bones and skulls. The moment I entered the room, he looked up at me with an annoyed, even hostile expression on his face.

"Weren't you ever taught to knock?" he said.

"I'm looking for the Rabbi."

"The Rabbi's gone," he said impatiently, pursing his lips and glaring at me as though I were an idiot. "All the Jews cleared out two days ago."

"What are you talking about?"

"The Jews cleared out two days ago," he repeated, letting out a disgusted sigh. "The Jansenists are going tomorrow, and the Jesuits are due to leave on Monday. Don't you know anything?"

"I don't have the slightest idea what you're talking about."

"The new laws. Religious groups have lost their academy

112

status. I can't believe that anyone could be so ignorant."

"You don't have to be nasty about it. Who do you think you are, anyway?"

"The name is Dujardin," he said. "Henri Dujardin. I'm an ethnographer."

"And this room belongs to you now?"

"Exactly. This room is mine."

"What about foreign journalists? Has their status changed, too?"

"I have no idea. That's not my concern."

"I suppose those bones and skulls are your concern."

"That's right. I'm in the process of analyzing them."

"Who did they belong to?"

"Anonymous corpses. People who froze to death."

"Do you know where the Rabbi is now?"

"On his way to the promised land, no doubt," he said sarcastically. "Now please go. You've taken up enough of my time. I have important work to do, and I don't like being interrupted. Thank you. And remember to close the door on your way out."

In the end, Sam and I never suffered from these laws. The failure of the Sea Wall Project had already weakened the government, and before they got around to the question of foreign journalists, a new regime came into power. The evictions of the religious groups had been no more than an absurd and desperate show of force, an arbitrary attack on those who were incapable of defending themselves. The utter uselessness of it stunned me, and it only made the Rabbi's disappearance that much harder to take. You see what things are like in this country. Everything disappears, people just as surely as objects, the living along with the dead. I mourned the loss of my friend, felt pulverized by the sheer weight of it. There was not even the certainty of death to console me—nothing more than a kind of blank, a ravening null.

After that, Sam's book became the most important thing in my life. As long as we kept working on it, I realized, the notion of a possible future would continue to exist for us. Sam had tried to explain that to me on the first day, but now I understood it for myself. I did whatever tasks needed to be done—classifying pages, editing the interviews, transcribing final versions, making a clean copy of the manuscript in longhand. It would have been better to have a typewriter, of course, but Sam had sold his portable several months earlier, and there was no way that we could afford to buy another. As it was, it was hard enough to maintain an adequate supply of pencils and pens. The winter shortages had driven up prices to record levels, and if not for the six pencils I already owned—as well as the two ballpoints I found by chance on the street—we might possibly have run out of materials. Paper we had in abundance (Sam had laid in a stock of twelve reams the day he moved in), but candles were another problem that interfered with our work. Daylight was necessary to us if we were to keep our expenses down, but there we were in the middle of winter, with the sun tracing its puny arc across the sky in just a few short hours, and unless we wanted the book to drag on forever, certain sacrifices had to be made. We tried to limit our smoking to four or five cigarettes a night, and eventually Sam let his beard grow out again. Razor blades were something of a luxury, after all, and it came down to a choice between a smooth face for him or smooth legs for me. The legs won hands down.

Day or night, candles were needed when going into the stacks. The books were located in the central core of the building, and consequently there were no windows in any of the walls. Since electric power had been shut off long ago, there was no choice but to carry your own light. At one time, they say, there had been more than a million volumes in the National Library. Those numbers had been vastly reduced by the time I got there, but hundreds of thousands still remained, a bewildering avalanche of print. Some books were standing upright on their shelves, some were strewn chaotically across the floor, still others were heaped into erratic piles. There was a strictly enforced library regulation against removing books from the building, but many had nevertheless been smuggled out and sold on the black market. It was debatable in any case whether the library was actually a library anymore. The system of classification had been thoroughly disrupted, and with so many books out of order, it was virtually impossible to find any volume you might have wanted. When you consider that there were seven floors of stacks, to say that a book was in the wrong place was as much to say that it had ceased to exist. Even though it might have been physically present in the building, the fact was that no one would ever find it again. I hunted down a number of old municipal registers for Sam, but most of my excursions into that place were simply to collect books at random. I didn't like being down there very much, never knowing who you might run into, having to smell all that clamminess and moldy decay. I would shove as many books as

I could under my two arms and then rush back to our room upstairs. The books were how we kept warm during the winter. In the absence of any other kind of fuel, we would burn them in the cast-iron stove for heat. I know it sounds like a terrible thing to have done, but we really didn't have much choice. It was either that or freeze to death. The irony does not escape me, of course—to have spent all those months working on a book and at the same time to have burned hundreds of other books to keep ourselves warm. The curious thing about it was that I never felt any regrets. To be honest, I actually think I enjoyed throwing those books into the flames. Perhaps it released some secret anger in me; perhaps it was simply a recognition of the fact that it did not matter what happened to them. The world they had belonged to was finished, and at least now they were being used to some purpose. Most of them were not worth opening anyway—sentimental novels, collections of political speeches, out-of-date textbooks. Whenever I found something that looked palatable, I would hold on to it and read it. Sometimes, when Sam was exhausted, I would read to him before he fell asleep. I remember going through parts of Herodotus that way, and one night I read the odd little book that Cyrano de Bergerac had written about his journeys to the moon and the sun. But in the end, everything made its way into the stove, everything went up in smoke.

Looking back on it now, I still believe that things could have worked out for us. We would have finished the book, and sooner or later we would have found a way to get home. If not for a stupid blunder I made just as the winter was ending, I might be sitting across from you now, telling you this story with my own voice. The fact that I made an innocent mistake does not lessen the pain of it. I should have known better, and because I acted impulsively, trusting someone I had no business to trust, I destroyed my entire life. I am not being dramatic when I say this. I destroyed everything with my own stupidity, and there is no one to blame but myself.

It happened like this. Shortly after the turn of the year, I discovered that I was pregnant. Not knowing how Sam would take the news, I kept it from him for a while, but then one day I was hit with a bad case of morning sickness—cold sweats, vomiting on the floor—and I wound up telling him the truth. Unbelievably, Sam was happy about it, perhaps even happier than I was. It's not that I didn't want the baby, you understand, but I couldn't help being frightened, and there were times when I could feel my nerve fail me, when the thought of giving birth to a child under those conditions struck me as madness. To the degree that I was worried, however, Sam was enthusiastic. He was positively invigorated by the idea of becoming a father, and little by little he soothed my doubts, got me to look at the pregnancy as a good omen. The child meant that we had been spared, he said. We had overturned the odds, and from now on everything would be different. By creating a child together, we had made it possible for a new world to begin. I had never heard Sam talk like this before. Such brave, idealistic sentiments—it almost shocked me to hear these things coming from him. But that does not mean I didn't love it. I loved it so much, I actually began to believe it myself.

More than anything, I did not want to let him down. In spite of a few bad mornings during the early weeks, my health remained good, and I tried to keep up my end of the work, just as I had done before. By mid-March, there were some signs that winter was beginning to lose its force: the storms struck a bit less often, the periods of thaw lasted a bit longer, the temperatures did not seem to drop so far at night. I don't mean to say that it had turned warm, but there were numerous little hints to suggest that things were moving in that direction, an ever-so-modest feeling that the worst was over. As luck would have it, it was just around this time that my shoes wore out—the same ones that Isabel had given me so long ago. I could not begin to calculate how many miles I had trekked in them. They had been with me for more than a year, absorbing every step I had taken, accompanying me into every corner of the city, and now they were completely shot: the soles had worn through, the uppers had turned to shreds, and even though I did my best to block up the holes with newspapers, the watery streets were too much for them, and inevitably my feet would get soaked whenever I went outside. This happened once too often, I suppose, and one day in early April I came down with a cold. It was the genuine article, complete with aches and chills, sore throat and sneezes, the whole parade. Given Sam's involvement with the pregnancy, this cold alarmed him to the point of hysteria. He dropped everything to take care of me, hovering around the bed like a demented nurse, throwing away money on extravagant items like tea and canned soups. I got better within three or four days, but afterward Sam laid down the law. Until we could find a new pair of shoes for me, he said, he didn't want me setting foot outside. He would do all the shopping and errands himself. I told him this was ridiculous, but he held his ground and refused to let me talk him out of it.

"Just because I'm pregnant, I don't want to be treated like an invalid," I said.

"It's not you," Sam said, "it's the shoes. Every time you go out, your feet are going to get wet. The next cold might not be so easy to cure, you know, and what would happen to us if you really got sick?"

"If you're so worried, why don't you give me your shoes to wear when I go out?"

"They're too big. You'd flop around in them like a child, and sooner or later you'd fall. Then what? The moment you hit the ground, someone would strip them off your feet."

"I can't help it if I have little feet. I was born that way."

"You have beautiful feet, Anna. The daintiest little twinkletoes ever invented. I worship at those feet. I kiss the ground they walk on. That's why they have to be protected. We have to make sure that no harm ever comes to them."

The next few weeks were difficult for me. I watched Sam waste his time on things I easily could have done myself, and the book made almost no progress. It galled me to think that a measly pair of shoes could cause so much trouble. The baby was just beginning to show then, and I felt like a useless cow, a numbskull princess who sat around indoors all day while her lord and knight went trudging into battle. If only I could find a pair of shoes, I kept telling myself, then life could get moving again. I began asking around a bit, questioning people while waiting in line at the sink, even going down to the Peripatetic Hours in the lobby a few times to see if anyone there could give me a lead. Nothing came of it, but then one day I ran into Dujardin in the sixth floor hallway, and he immediately launched into a conversation with me, chattering away as though we were old familiars. I had steered clear of Dujardin ever since our first meeting in the Rabbi's room, and this sudden friendliness on his part struck me as odd. Dujardin was a pedantic little weasel of a man, and for all these months he had avoided me just as carefully as I had avoided him. Now he was all smiles and sympathetic concern. "I've heard talk that you are in need of a pair of shoes," he said. "If that is correct, I might be in a position to offer you some help." I should have known something was wrong right away, but the mention of the word "shoes" threw me off. I was so desperate to get them, you understand, that it did not occur to me to question his motives.

"The thing of it is this," he rattled on. "I have a cousin who's connected with the, hmmm, how shall I put it, with the business of buying and selling. Usable objects, you know, consumer articles, things of that sort. Shoes sometimes cross his path—the ones I am wearing now, for example—and I don't think it would be amiss to assume that he has others in stock at this moment. Since I happen to be going to his house tonight, it would be nothing, absolutely nothing, for me to make some inquiries on your behalf. I will need to know your size, of course—hmmm, not large I shouldn't think—and how much you are willing to spend. But those are details, mere details. If we can set a time to meet tomorrow, I might have some information for you then. Everyone needs shoes, after all, and from the looks of what you have on your feet now, I can understand why you've been asking around. Rags and tatters. It just won't do, not with the weather we have these days."

I told him my size, the money I could spend, and then fixed an appointment for the following afternoon. Unctuous as he was, I couldn't help feeling that Dujardin was trying to be nice. He probably took a cut from the business he drummed up for his cousin, but I didn't find anything wrong with that. We all have to make money somehow, and if he had a scheme or two cooking on the side, then so much the better for him. I managed to say nothing to Sam about this encounter for the rest of the day. It was by no means sure that Dujardin's cousin would have anything for me, but if the deal worked out, I wanted it to be a surprise. I did my best not to count on it. Our funds had dwindled to less than a hundred glots by then, and the figure I had mentioned to Dujardin was absurdly low— just eleven or twelve glots, I think, maybe even ten. On the other hand, he hadn't blinked at my offer, and that seemed to be a sign of encouragement. It was enough to keep my hopes up anyway, and for the next twenty-four hours I spun in a turmoil of anticipation.

We met in the northwest corner of the main lobby at two o'clock the next day. Dujardin showed up carrying a brown paper bag, and the moment I saw it I knew that things had gone well. "I believe we're in luck," he said, taking my arm conspiratorially and leading me behind a marble column where no one could see us. "My cousin had a pair in your size, and he's willing to sell them for thirteen glots. I'm sorry I couldn't get the price down any lower, but that was the best I could do. Given the quality of the merchandise, it still stands as an excellent bargain." Turning in to the wall so that his back was facing me, Dujardin cautiously pulled a shoe from the bag. It was a brown leather walking shoe for the left foot. The materials were obviously genuine, and the sole was made of a durable, comfortable-looking hard rubber—perfect for negotiating the streets of the city. What was more, the shoe was in nearly pristine condition.

"Try it on," Dujardin said. "Let's see if it fits." It did. As I stood there wiggling my toes along the smooth inner sole, I felt happier than I had in a long time. "You've saved my life," I said. "For thirteen glots we have ourselves a deal. Just give me the other shoe, and I'll pay you right now." But Dujardin seemed to hesitate, and then, with an embarrassed look on his face, showed me that the bag was empty. "Is this some kind of joke?" I said. "Where's the other shoe?"

"I don't have it with me," he said.

"It's all a wretched little come-on, isn't it? You dangle a good shoe in front of my nose, get me to give you money for the pair in advance, and then present me with a beat-up piece of junk for the other foot. Isn't that right? Well, I'm sorry, but I'm not going to fall for that trick. There won't be a single glot from me until I see the other shoe."

"No, Miss Blume, you don't understand. It's not like that at all. The other shoe is in the same condition as this one, and no one is asking you for money in advance. It's my cousin's way of doing business, I'm afraid. He insisted that you go to his office in person to complete the transaction. I tried to talk him out of it, but he wouldn't listen to me. At such a low price, he said, there was no room for a middleman."

"Are you trying to tell me that your cousin doesn't trust you for thirteen glots?"

"It puts me in a very awkward position, I admit. But my cousin is a hard man. He doesn't trust anyone when it comes to business. You can imagine how I felt when he told me this. He cast my integrity into doubt, and that is a bitter pill to swallow, I can assure you."

"If there's nothing in it for you, then why did you bother to keep our appointment?"

"I had made you a promise, Miss Blume, and I didn't want to renege. That only would have proved my cousin right, and I have my dignity to think of, you know, I have my pride. Those are things more important than money."

Dujardin's performance was impressive. There was no flaw in it, not the slightest crack to suggest that he was anything other than a man whose feelings had been deeply hurt. I thought: he wants to stay in his cousin's good graces, and therefore he is willing to do me this favor. It's a test for him, and if he manages to pass it successfully, his cousin will begin allowing him to make deals on his own. You see how clever I was trying to be. I thought I had outsmarted Dujardin, and because of that, I did not have the sense to be afraid.

It was a sparkling afternoon. Sunlight everywhere, and the wind all but carrying us in its arms. I felt like someone who had recovered from a long illness—experiencing that light again, feeling my legs as they moved below me in the open air. We walked at a brisk tempo, dodging numerous impediments, veering nimbly around the heaps of wreckage left by winter, and barely exchanged a word the whole way. Spring was definitely on the verge now, but patches of snow and ice were still present in the shadows that jutted from the sides of buildings, and out in the streets, where the sun was strongest, broad rivers rushed among the churned-up stones and crumbling bits of pavement. My shoes were a sorry mess after ten minutes, inside as well as out: socks drenched through, toes all damp and slippery from the cool seepage. It's odd to be mentioning these details now, perhaps, but they are what stand out most vividly from that day—the happiness of the journey, the buoyant, almost drunken sense of movement. Afterward, when we got to where we were going, things happened too fast for me to remember them. If I see them now, it is only in short, random clusters, isolated images removed from any context, bursts of light and shadow. The building, for example, left no impression on me. I remember that it was on the edge of the warehouse district in the eighth census zone, not far from where Ferdinand had once had his sign studio—but that was only because Isabel had once pointed out the street to me in passing, and I sensed that I was on familiar ground. It could be that I was too distracted to take in the surfaces of things, too lost in my own thoughts to be thinking about anything except how glad Sam would be when I returned. As a consequence, the facade of the building is a blank to me. Likewise the act of walking through the front door and climbing several flights of stairs. It's as if those things never happened, even though I know for a fact they did. The first image that comes to me with any clarity is the face of Dujardin's cousin. Not so much his face, perhaps, but my noticing that he wore the same wire-rimmed glasses as Dujardin, and my wondering—ever so briefly, for the merest prick of a moment—if they had bought them from the same person. I don't think I actually had my eyes on that face for more than a second or two, for just then, as he came forward to shake my hand, a door opened behind him—accidentally, it would seem, for the noise of it turning on its hinges changed his expression from one of cordiality to sudden, desperate concern, and he immediately turned around to close it without bothering to shake my hand—and in that instant I understood that I had been deceived, that my visit to this place had nothing to do with shoes or money or business of any kind. For right then, in the tiny interval that elapsed before he shut the door again, I was able to see clearly into the other room, and there was no mistaking what I saw in there: three or four human bodies hanging naked from meat-hooks, and another man with a hatchet leaning over a table and lopping off the limbs of another corpse. There had been rumors circulating in the library that human slaughter-houses now existed, but I hadn't believed them. Now, because the door behind Dujardin's cousin had accidentally slipped open, I was able to glimpse the fate these men had planned for me. At that point, I think I started to scream. At times I can even hear myself shouting the word "murderers" over and over again. But that couldn't have gone on for very long. It's impossible to reconstruct my thoughts from that moment, impossible to know if I was thinking anything at all. I saw a window to my left and ran for it. I remember seeing Dujardin and his cousin make a lunge for me, but I ran through their outstretched arms at full tilt and went crashing through the window. I remember the sound of the glass shattering and the air rushing into my face. It must have been a long drop. Long enough for me to realize that I was falling, at any rate. Long enough for me to know that once I hit the bottom, I would be dead.

Little by little, I am trying to tell you what happened. I can't help it if there are gaps in my memory. Certain events refuse to reappear, and no matter how hard I struggle, I am powerless to unearth them. I must have passed out the moment I made contact with the ground, but I have no memory of pain, no memory of where I fell. When it comes right down to it, the only thing I can be certain of is that I did not die. This is a fact that continues to confound me. More than two years after my fall from that window, I still don't understand how I managed to live.

I groaned when they lifted me, they said, but afterward I remained inert, barely breathing anymore, barely making any sound at all. A long time passed. They never told me how long, but I gather it was more than a day, perhaps as many as three or four. When I finally opened my eyes, they said, it was less a recovery than a resurrection, an absolute rising up out of nothingness. I remember noticing a ceiling above me and wondering how I had got myself indoors, but an instant later I was stabbed by pain—in my head, along my right side, in my belly—and it hurt so much that I gasped. I was in a bed, a real bed with sheets and pillows, but all I could do was lie there, whimpering as the pain traveled through my body. A woman suddenly appeared in my field of vision, looking down at me with a smile on her face. She was about thirty-eight or forty, with dark wavy hair and large green eyes. In spite of how I was feeling at that moment, I could see that she was beautiful—perhaps the most beautiful woman I had seen since coming to the city.

"It must hurt a lot," she said.

"You don't have to smile about it," I answered. "I'm not in the mood for smiles." God knows where I developed this sense of tact, but the pain was so wretched that I spoke the first words that came into my head. The woman did not seem put off, however, and went on smiling the same comforting smile.

"I'm glad to see that you're alive," she said.

126

"You mean I'm not dead? You'll have to prove that to me before I believe it."

"You have a broken arm, a couple of broken ribs, and a bad bump on the head. For the time being, however, it seems that you're alive. That tongue of yours is proof enough, I should think."

"Who are you, anyway," I said, refusing to give up my petulance. "The angel of mercy?"

"I'm Victoria Woburn. And this is Woburn House. We help people here."

"Beautiful women aren't allowed to be doctors. It's against the rules."

"I'm not a doctor. My father was, but he's dead now. He was the one who started Woburn House."

"I heard someone talk about this place once. I thought he was making it up."

"That happens. It's hard to know what to believe anymore."

"Are you the one who brought me here?"

"No, Mr. Frick did. Mr. Frick and his grandson, Willie. They go out in the car every Wednesday afternoon to make the rounds. Not all the people who need help can get here by themselves, you understand, so we go out and find them. We try to take in at least one new person that way every week."

"You mean they found me by accident?"

"They were driving by when you went crashing through that window."

"I wasn't trying to kill myself," I said defensively. "You shouldn't get any funny ideas about that."

"Leapers don't jump from windows. And when they do, they make sure to open them first."

127

"I would never kill myself," I said, blustering on to emphasize the point, but just as I spoke these words, a dark truth began to dawn in me. "I would never kill myself," I said again. "I'm going to have a baby, you see, and why would a pregnant woman want to kill herself? She'd have to be insane to do a thing like that."

From the way her face changed expression, I immediately knew what had happened. I knew it without having to be told. My baby was no longer inside me. The fall had been too much for it, and now it was dead. I can't tell you how bleak everything became at that moment. It was a raw, animal misery that took hold of me, and there were no images inside it, no thoughts, absolutely nothing to see or think. I must have begun crying before she said another word.

"It's a miracle that you managed to get pregnant in the first place," she said, stroking my cheek with her hand. "Babies don't get born here anymore. You know that as well as I do. It hasn't happened in years."

"I don't care," I said angrily, trying to talk through my sobs. "You're wrong. My baby was going to live. I know that my baby was going to live."

Each time my chest convulsed, my ribs were scorched with pain. I tried to stifle these outbursts, but that only made them more intense. I shook from the effort to keep myself still, and that in turn unleashed a series of unendurable spasms. Victoria tried to comfort me, but I didn't want her comfort. I didn't want anyone's comfort. "Please go away," I finally said. "I don't want anyone to be here now. You've been very kind to me, but I need to be left alone."

It took a long time before my injuries got better. The cuts on my face cleared up without much permanent damage (a scar on my forehead and another close to the temple), and my ribs mended in due course. The broken arm did not knit smoothly, however, and it still gives me a fair amount of trouble: pain whenever I move it too brusquely or in the wrong direction, an inability to extend it fully anymore. The bandages stayed on my head for almost a month, the bumps and scrapes subsided, but since then I have been left with something of a headache condition: knife-like migraines that attack at random moments, an occasional dull ache throbbing at the back of my skull. As far as the other blows are concerned, I hesitate to talk about them. My womb is an enigma, and I have no way of measuring the catastrophe that took place inside it.

The physical damage was only part of the problem, however. Just hours after my first conversation with Victoria, there was more bad news, and at that point I nearly gave up, I nearly stopped wanting to live. Early that evening she came back to my room with a tray of food. I told her how urgent it was for someone to go to the National Library and find Sam. He would be worried to death, I said, and I needed to be with him now. *Now*, I screamed, I need to be with him *now*. I was suddenly beside myself, sobbing out of control. Willie, the fifteen-year-old boy, was dispatched on the errand, but the news he brought back was devastating. A fire had broken out in the library that afternoon, he said, and the roof had already collapsed. No one knew how it had started, but the building was totally in flames by now, and word was that over a hundred people were trapped inside. It was still unclear whether anyone had managed to escape; there were rumors pro and con. But even if Sam had been one of the fortunate ones, there was no way that Willie or anyone else would be able to find him. And if he had died along with the others, then everything was lost for me. I saw no way around it. If he was dead, then I had no right to be alive. And if he was alive, then it was almost certain that I would never see him again.

Those were the facts I had to deal with during my first months at Woburn House. It was a dark period for me, darker than any period I have ever known. In the beginning, I stayed in the room upstairs. Three times a day someone would come to visit me—twice to deliver meals, once to empty the chamber pot. There was always a commotion of people down below (voices, shuffling feet, groans and laughter, howls, snoring at night), but I was too weak and depressed to bother getting out of bed. I moped and sulked, brooded under the blankets, wept without warning. Spring had come by then, and I spent most of my time looking at the clouds through the window, inspecting the molding that ran along the top of the walls, staring at the cracks in the ceiling. For the first ten or twelve days, I don't think I even managed to go into the hallway outside the door.

Woburn House was a five-story mansion with over twenty rooms—set back from the street and surrounded by a small private park. It had been built by Dr. Woburn's grandfather nearly a hundred years before and was considered to be one of the most elegant private residences in the city. When the period of troubles began, Dr. Woburn was among the first to call attention to the growing numbers of homeless people. Because he was a respected doctor from an important family, his statements were given a good deal of publicity, and it soon became fashionable in wealthy circles to support his cause. There were fund-raising dinners, charity dances, and other society functions, and ultimately a number of buildings around the city were converted into shelters. Dr. Woburn gave up his private practice to administer these way houses, as they were called, and every morning he would go out in his chauffeur-driven car to visit them, talking to the people who lived there and giving whatever medical assistance he could. He became something of a legend in the city, known for his goodness and idealism, and whenever people talked about the barbarity of the times, his name was brought up to prove that noble actions were still possible. But that was long ago, before anyone believed that things could disintegrate to the extent they finally did. As conditions grew worse, the success of Dr. Woburn's project was gradually undermined. The homeless population grew in vast, geometric surges, and the money to finance the shelters dwindled at an equal rate. Rich people absconded, stealing out of the country with their gold and diamonds, and those who remained could no longer afford to be generous. The doctor spent large sums of his own money on the shelters, but that did not prevent them from failing, and one by one they had to shut their doors. Another man might have given up, but he refused to let the matter end there. If he could not save thousands, he said, then perhaps he could save hundreds, and if he could not save hundreds, then perhaps he could save twenty or thirty. The numbers were no longer important. Too much had happened by then, and he knew that any help he could offer would only be symbolic—a gesture against total ruin. That was six or seven years ago, and Dr. Woburn was already well past sixty. With his daughter's support, he decided to open up his house to strangers, converting the first two floors of the family mansion into a combination hospital and shelter. Beds were bought, kitchen supplies were bought, and little by little they worked their way through the remaining assets of the Woburn fortune to maintain the operation. When the cash was exhausted, they began selling off heirlooms and antiques, gradually emptying the upstairs rooms of their contents. With constant, back-breaking effort, they were able to house from eighteen to twenty-four people at any given time. Indigents were allowed to stay for ten days; the desperately ill could stay longer. Everyone was given a clean bed and two warm meals a day. Nothing was solved by this, of course, but at least people were given a respite from their troubles, a chance to gather strength before moving on. "We can't do much," the doctor would say. "But the little we can do we are doing."

Dr. Woburn had been dead for just four months when I arrived at Woburn House. Victoria and the others were doing their best to carry on without him, but certain changes had been necessary—particularly with the medical aspect of things, since there was no one who could do the doctor's work. Both Victoria and Mr. Frick were competent nurses, but that was a far cry from being able to diagnose ailments and prescribe treatments. I think that helps to explain why I received such special attention from them. Of all the injured people who had been brought in since the doctor's death, I was the first one who had responded to their care, the first one who had shown any signs of recovery. In that sense, I served to justify their determination to keep Woburn House open. I was their success story, the shining example of what they were still able to accomplish, and for that reason they coddled me for as long as I seemed to demand it, indulged me in my black moods, gave me every benefit of the doubt.

Mr. Frick believed that I had actually risen from the dead. He had worked as the doctor's chauffeur for a long time (forty-one years, he told me), and he had seen more of life and death at close quarters than most people ever do. To hear him tell it, there had never been such a case as mine. "No sir, miss," he would say. "You was already in the other world. I seed it with my own eyes. You was dead, and then you come back to life." Mr. Frick had an odd, ungrammatical way of speaking, and he often made a hash of his ideas when trying to express them. I don't think this had anything to do with the quality of his mind—it was simply that words gave him trouble. He had difficulty maneuvering them around his tongue, and he would sometimes stumble over them as though they were physical objects, literal stones cluttering his mouth. Because of this, he seemed especially sensitive to the internal properties of words themselves: their sounds as divorced from their meanings, their symmetries and contradictions. "Words be what tells me how to know," he once explained to me. "That's why I got to be such an old man. My name is Otto. It go back and forth the same. It don't end nowhere but begin again. I get to live twice that way, twice as long as no one else. You too, miss. You be named the same as me. A-n-n-a. Back and forth the same, just like Otto myself. That's why you got to be born again. It's a blessing of luck, Miss Anna. You was dead,

133

and I seed you get born again with my own eyes. It's a great good blessing of luck."

There was a stolid grace to this old man, with his thin, spiny erectness and ivory-colored jowls. His loyalty to Dr. Woburn was unswerving, and even now he continued to maintain the car he had driven for him—an ancient, sixteen-cylinder Pierce Arrow with running boards and leather-upholstered seats. This black, fifty-year-old automobile had been the doctor's only eccentricity, and every Tuesday night, no matter how much other work had to be done, Frick would go out to the garage behind the house and spend at least two hours polishing and cleaning it, putting it into the best possible shape for the Wednesday afternoon rounds. He had adapted the engine to run on methane gas, and this cleverness with his hands was surely the chief reason why Woburn House had not fallen apart. He had repaired plumbing, installed showers, dug a new well. These and sundry other improvements had kept the place functioning through the hardest of times. His grandson, Willie, worked as his assistant on all these projects, silently following him around from one job to another, a morose and stunted little figure in a green hooded sweatshirt. Frick's plan was to teach the boy enough so that he could take over for him after he died, but Willie did not seem to be an especially fast learner. "Nothing to worry," Frick said to me one day on this subject. "We break in Willie slow. There's no rush about it no how. By the time I get ready to kick the bucket, the boy be growed into an old man, too."

It was Victoria who took the greatest interest in me, however. I have mentioned how important my recovery was to her, but I think there was more to it than that. She was hungry for someone to talk to, and as my strength gradually returned, she began coming upstairs to see me more often. Ever since her father's death, she had been alone with Frick and Willie, running the shelter and attending to business, but there had been no one for her to share her thoughts with. Little by little, I seemed to become that person. It was not difficult for us to talk to each other, and as our friendship developed, I understood how much we had in common. It is true that I did not come from the same kind of wealth that Victoria did, but my childhood had been an easy one, filled with bourgeois splendors and advantages, and I had lived with a sense that all my desires were within the realm of possibility. I had gone to good schools and was capable of discussing books. I knew the difference between a Beaujolais and a Bordeaux, and I understood why Schubert was a greater musician than Schumann. Given the world that Victoria had been born into at Woburn House, I was probably closer to being a member of her own class than anyone she had met in years. I don't meant to suggest that Victoria was a snob. Money itself did not interest her, and she had turned her back on the things it represented long ago. It's just that we shared a certain language, and when she talked to me about her past, I understood her without having to ask for explanations.

She had been married twice—once briefly, in a "brilliant society match," as she sarcastically put it, and the next time to a man she referred to as Tommy, although I never learned his last name. He had apparently been a lawyer, and together they had had two children, a girl and a boy. When the Troubles began, he had been increasingly drawn into politics, working first as under-secretary for the Green Party (at one time, all political affiliations here were designated by colors), and then, when the Blue Party absorbed the membership of his organization in a strategic alliance, as urban coordinator for the western half of the city. At the time of the first Anti-Tollist uprisings eleven or twelve years ago, he was trapped in one of the riots along Nero Prospect and shot down by a policeman's bullet. After Tommy's death, her father urged her to leave the country with the children (who were just three and four at the time), but Victoria refused. Instead, she sent them along with Tommy's parents to live in England. She did not want to be one of those people who had given up and run away, she said, but neither did she want to subject her children to the disasters that were bound to come. There are some decisions that no one should ever be forced to make, I believe, choices that simply put too great a burden on the mind. Whatever it is you finally do, you are going to regret it, and you will go on regretting it for as long as you live. The children went off to England, and for the next year or two Victoria managed to keep in touch with them by mail. Then the postal system began to break down. Communications became sporadic and unpredictable—a constant anguish of waiting, of messages thrown out blindly to sea—and at last they stopped altogether. That was eight years ago. Not one word had arrived since, and Victoria was long past hoping that she would ever hear from them again.

I mention these things to show you the similarities between our experiences, the links that helped to form our friendship. The people she loved were gone from her life just as terribly as the people I loved were gone from mine. Our husbands and children, her father and my brother—all of them had vanished into death and uncertainty. When I was well enough to go, therefore (but where did I really

136

have to go?), it seemed only natural that she should invite me to stay on at Woburn House to work as a member of the staff. It was not a solution I would have wished for myself, but under the circumstances I saw no other choice. The do-gooder philosophy of the place made me a bit uncomfortable—the idea of helping strangers, of sacrificing yourself to a cause. The principle was too abstract for me, too earnest, too altruistic. Sam's book had been something for me to believe in, but Sam had been my darling, my life, and I wondered if I had it in me to devote myself to people I didn't know. Victoria saw my reluctance, but she did not argue with me or try to change my mind. More than anything else, I think it was this restraint of hers that led me to accept. She did not make a big speech or try to convince me that I was about to save my soul. She simply said: "There's a lot of work to be done here, Anna, more work than we can ever hope to do. I have no idea what will happen in your case, but broken hearts are sometimes mended by work."

The routine was endless and exhausting. This was not a cure so much as a distraction, but anything that dulled the ache was welcome to me. I wasn't expecting miracles, after all. I had already used up my supply of those, and I knew that everything from now on would be aftermath—a dreadful, posthumous sort of life, a life that would go on happening to me, even though it was finished. The ache, then, did not disappear. But little by little I began to notice that I was crying less, that I did not necessarily drench the pillow before I fell asleep at night, and once I even discovered that I had managed to go three straight hours without thinking of Sam. These were small triumphs, I admit, but given what things were like for me then, I was in no position to scoff at them.

There were six rooms downstairs with three or four beds in each. The second floor had two private rooms set aside for difficult cases, and it was in one of those that I had spent my first weeks at Woburn House. After I started working, I was given my own bedroom on the fourth floor. Victoria's room was down the hall, and Frick and Willie lived in a large room directly above hers. The only other person on the staff lived downstairs, in a room just off the kitchen. That was Maggie Vine, a deaf-mute woman of no particular age who served as the cook and laundress. She was very short, with thick, stumpy thighs and a broad face crowned by a jungle of red hair. Other than the conversations she held in sign language with Victoria, she did not communicate with anyone. She went about her work in a kind of sullen trance, doggedly and efficiently completing every job that was assigned to her, working such long hours that I wondered if she ever slept. She rarely greeted me or acknowledged my presence, but every now and again, on those occasions when we happened to be alone together, she would tap me on the shoulder, break into an enormous smile, and then proceed to give an elaborate pantomime performance of an opera singer delivering an aria—complete with histrionic gestures and quivering throat. Then she would bow, graciously acknowledging the cheers from her imaginary audience, and abruptly return to work, without any pause or transition. It was perfectly mad. This must have happened six or seven times, but I could never tell if she was trying to amuse me or frighten me. In all the years she had been there, Victoria said, Maggie had never sung for anyone else.

Every resident, as we called them, had to agree to certain conditions before being allowed to stay at Woburn House. No fighting or stealing, for example, and a willingness to pitch in with the chores: making one's bed, carrying one's plate to the kitchen after meals, and so on. In exchange, the residents were given room and board, a new set of clothes, an opportunity to shower every day, and unlimited use of the facilities. These included the downstairs parlor— which featured a number of sofas and easy chairs, a well-stocked library, and games of various sorts (cards, bingo, backgammon)—as well as the yard behind the house, which was a particularly pleasant place to be when the weather was good. There was a croquet field out there in the far corner, a badminton net, and a large selection of lawn chairs. By any standard, Woburn House was a haven, an idyllic refuge from the misery and squalor around it. You would think that anyone given the chance to spend a few days in such a place would relish every moment of it, but that did not always seem to be true. Most were grateful, of course, most appreciated what was being done for them, but there were many others who had a difficult time of it. Disputes among residents were common, and it seemed that just about anything could set them off: the way someone ate his food or picked his nose, the opinion of this one as opposed to that one, the way someone coughed or snored while everyone else was trying to sleep—all the petty squabbles that occur when people are suddenly thrown together under one roof. There is nothing unusual about that, I suppose, but I always found it rather pathetic, a sad and ridiculous little farce that was played out again and again. Nearly all the residents of Woburn House had been living in the streets for a long time. Perhaps the contrast between that life and this life was too much of a shock for them. You grow accustomed to looking out for yourself, to thinking only of your own welfare, and then someone tells you that you have to cooperate with a bunch of strangers, the very class of people you have taught yourself to mistrust. Since you know that you will be back on the streets in just a few short days, is it really worth the trouble to dismantle your personality for that?

Other residents seemed almost disappointed by what they found at Woburn House. These were the ones who had waited so long to be admitted that their expectations had been exaggerated beyond reason—turning Woburn House into an earthly paradise, the object of every possible longing they had ever felt. The idea of being allowed to live there had kept them going from one day to the next, but once they actually got in, they were bound to experience a letdown. They were not entering an enchanted realm, after all. Woburn House was a lovely place to be, but it was nevertheless in the real world, and what you found there was only more life—a better life, perhaps, but still no more than life as you had always known it. The remarkable thing was how quickly everyone adapted to the material comforts that were offered—the beds and showers, the good food and clean clothes, the chance to do nothing. After two or three days at Woburn House, men and women who had been eating out of garbage cans could sit down to a large spread at an attractively set table with all the aplomb and composure of fat, middle-class burghers. Perhaps that is not as strange as it seems. We all take things

140

for granted, and when it comes to such basic things as food and shelter, things that are probably ours by natural right, then it doesn't take long for us to think of them as an integral part of ourselves. It is only when we lose them that we ever notice the things we had. As soon as we get them back, we stop noticing them again. That was the problem with the people who felt let down by Woburn House. They had lived with deprivation for so long that they could think of nothing else, but once they got back the things they had lost, they were amazed to discover that no great change had taken place in them. The world was just as it had always been. Their bellies were full now, but nothing else had been altered in the least.

We were always careful to warn people about the difficulties of the last day, but I don't think our advice ever did anyone much good. You can't prepare yourself for something like that, and there was no way for us to predict who would balk at the crucial moment and who would not. Some people were able to leave without trauma, but others could not bring themselves to face it. They suffered horribly at the thought of having to return to the streets—especially the kind ones, the gentle ones, the people who were most grateful for the help we had given them—and there were times when I seriously questioned whether any of it was worth it, whether it would not in fact have been better to do nothing than to hold out gifts to people and then snatch them out of their hands a moment later. There was a fundamental cruelty to the process, and more often than not I found it intolerable. To watch grown men and women suddenly fall to their knees and beg you for one more day. To witness the tears, the howls, the berserk supplications. Some feigned illnesses—falling into dead swoons, pre-

tending to be paralyzed—and others went so far as to in-
jure themselves on purpose: slashing their wrists, gouging
their legs with scissors, amputating fingers and toes. Then,
at the very limit, there were the suicides, at least three or
four that I can remember. We were supposed to be helping
people at Woburn House, but there were times when we
actually destroyed them.

The quandary is immense, however. The moment you
accept the idea that there might be some good in a place
like Woburn House, you sink into a swamp of contradictions. It is not enough simply to argue that residents should
be allowed to stay longer—particularly if you mean to be
fair. What about all the others who are standing outside,
waiting for a chance to get in? For every person who occupied a bed in Woburn House, there were dozens more
begging to be admitted. What is better—to help large numbers of people a little bit or small numbers of people a lot?
I don't really think there is an answer to this question. Dr.
Woburn had started the enterprise in a certain way, and
Victoria was determined to stick with it to the end. That
did not necessarily make it right. But it did not make it
wrong either. The problem did not lie in the method so
much as in the nature of the problem itself. There were
too many people to be helped and not enough people to
help them. The arithmetic was overpowering, inexorable
in the havoc it produced. No matter how hard you worked,
there was no chance you were not going to fail. That was
the long and the short of it. Unless you were willing to
accept the utter futility of the job, there was no point in
going on with it.

Most of my time was taken up with interviewing pro-
spective residents, putting their names on a list, organizing

the schedules of who would be moving in and when. The interviews were held from nine in the morning to one in the afternoon, and on the average I spoke to twenty or twenty-five people a day. I saw them separately, one after the other, in the front hallway of the house. There had apparently been some ugly incidents in the past—violent attacks, groups of people trying to storm through the door— and so there always had to be an armed guard on duty while the interviews were taking place. Frick would stand out on the front steps with a rifle, watching the crowd to make sure the line advanced smoothly and things did not get out of control. The numbers outside the house could be breathtaking, particularly during the warm months. It was not uncommon for fifty to seventy-five people to be out there on the street at any given moment. This meant that most of the people I saw had been waiting from three to six days just for a chance to be interviewed—sleeping on the sidewalk, inching their way forward in the line, stubbornly hanging on until their turn finally came. One by one, they stumbled in to see me, an endless, unremitting flow of people. They would sit down in the red leather chair on the other side of the table from me, and I would ask them all the necessary questions. Name, age, marital status, former occupation, last permanent address, and so on. That never took more than a couple of minutes, but it was the rare interview that stopped at that point. They all wanted to tell me their stories, and I had no choice but to listen. It was a different story every time, and yet each story was finally the same. The strings of bad luck, the miscalculations, the growing weight of circumstances. Our lives are no more than the sum of manifold contingencies, and no matter how diverse they might be in their details, they all share an essential randomness in their design: this then that, and because of that, this. One day I woke up and saw. I'd hurt my leg and so I couldn't run fast enough. My wife said, my mother fell, my husband forgot. I heard hundreds of these stories, and there were times when I didn't think I could stand it anymore. I had to be sympathetic, to nod in all the right places, but the placid, professional manner I tried to maintain was a poor defense against the things I heard. I was not cut out for listening to the stories of girls who had worked as prostitutes in the Euthanasia Clinics. I had no talent for listening to mothers tell me how their children had died. It was too gruesome, too unrelenting, and it was all I could do to hide behind the mask of the job. I would put the person's name down on the list and give him a date—two, three, even four months off. We should have a spot for you then, I would say. When the time came for them to move into Woburn House, I was the one who checked them in. That was my principal job in the afternoons: showing the newcomers around, explaining the rules, helping them to get settled. Most of them managed to keep the appointments I had set for them so many weeks earlier, but there were some who failed to show up. It was never very hard to guess the reason. The policy was to hold that person's bed open for one full day. If he did not show up then, I would remove his name from the list.

The Woburn House supplier was a man named Boris Stepanovich. He was the one who brought us the food we needed, the bars of soap, the towels, the odd piece of equipment. He showed up as often as four or five times a week, delivering the things we had asked for and then carrying off yet another treasure from the Woburn estate: a china teapot, a set of antimacassars, a violin or picture frame—all the objects that had been stored in the fifth-floor rooms and that continued to provide the cash that kept Woburn House running. Boris Stepanovich had been on the scene for a long time, Victoria told me, ever since the period of Dr. Woburn's original shelters. The two men had apparently known each other for many years before that, and given what I had learned about the doctor, it surprised me that he should have been friends with such a dubious character as Boris Stepanovich. I believe it had something to do with the fact that the doctor had once saved Boris's life, but it might have been the other way around. I heard several different versions of the story and could never be sure which one was true.

Boris Stepanovich was a plump, middle-aged man who seemed almost fat by the standards of the city. He had a taste for flamboyant clothes (fur hats, walking sticks, boutonierres), and in his round, leathery face there was something that reminded me of an Indian chief or Oriental potentate. Everything he did had a certain flair to it, even the way he smoked cigarettes—holding them tightly between his thumb and index finger, inhaling the smoke with an elegant, upside-down nonchalance, and then releasing it through his bulky nostrils like steam from a boiling kettle. It was often difficult to follow him in conversation, however, and as I got to know him better, I learned to expect a good deal of confusion whenever Boris Stepanovich opened his mouth. He was fond of obscure pronouncements and elliptical allusions, and he embellished simple remarks with such ornate imagery that you soon got lost trying to understand him. Boris had an aversion to being pinned down, and he used language as an instrument of locomotion—constantly on the move, darting and feinting, circling, disappearing, suddenly appearing again in a different spot. At one time or another, he told me so many stories about himself, presented so many conflicting accounts of his life, that I gave up trying to believe anything. One day, he would assure me that he had been born in the city and had lived there all his life. The next day, as if having forgotten his previous story, he would tell me that he had been born in Paris and was the oldest son of Russian émigrés. Then, shifting course yet again, he would confess to me that Boris Stepanovich was not his real name. Owing to some unpleasant difficulties with the Turkish police in his youth, he had taken on another identity. Since then, he had changed his name so many times that he could no longer remember what his real name was. No matter, he said. A man must live from moment to moment, and who cares what you were last month if you know who you are today? Originally, he said, he had been an Algonquin Indian, but after his father died, his mother had married a Russian count. He himself had never married, or else he had been married three times—depending on which version served his purpose at the moment. Whenever Boris Stepanovich launched into one of his personal histories, it was always to prove some point or other—as if by resorting to his own experience he could claim final authority on any given subject. For that reason he had also held every imaginable job, from the humblest manual work to the most exalted executive position. He had been a dishwasher, a juggler, a car salesman, a literature professor, a pickpocket, a real estate broker, a newspaper editor, and the manager of a large department store that specialized in women's fashions. I am no doubt forgetting others, but you begin to get the idea. Boris Stepanovich never really expected you to believe what he said, but at the same time he did not treat his inventions as lies. They were part of an almost conscious plan to concoct a more pleasant world for himself—a world that could shift according to his whims, that was not subject to the same laws and bleak necessities that dragged down all the rest of us. If this did not make him a realist in the strict sense of the word, he was not one to delude himself either. Boris Stepanovich was not quite the conniving blowhard he appeared to be, and underneath his bluff and heartiness there was always a hint of something else—an acumen, perhaps, a sense of some deeper understanding. I would not go so far as to say that he was a good person (not in the sense that Isabel and Victoria were good), but Boris had his own set of rules and he stuck to them. Unlike everyone else I had met here, he managed to float above his circumstances. Starvation, murder, the worst forms of cruelty—he walked right by them, even through them, and yet always appeared unscathed. It was as though he had imagined every possibility in advance, and therefore he was never surprised by what happened. Inherent in this attitude was a pessimism so deep, so devastating, so fully in tune with the facts, that it actually made him cheerful.

Once or twice a week, Victoria would ask me to accompany Boris Stepanovich on his rounds through the city—his "buy-sell expeditions," as he called them. It's not that I was able to help him very much, but I was always happy for the chance to leave my work, even if only for a few hours. Victoria understood that, I think, and she was careful not to push me too hard. My mood remained low, and for the most part I continued to be in a fragile state of mind—easily upset, grumpy and uncommunicative for no apparent reason. Boris Stepanovich was probably good medicine for me, and I began looking forward to our little excursions as a break from the monotony of my thoughts.

I was never a party to Boris's buying trips (where he found the food for Woburn House and how he managed to locate the things we ordered from him), but I often observed him as he went about the business of selling the objects that Victoria had chosen to liquidate. He took a ten percent cut from these deals, but to watch him in action you would have thought he was working entirely for himself. Boris made it a rule never to go to the same Resurrection Agent more than once a month. As a consequence, we ranged widely over the city, setting off in a new direction each time, often wandering into territories I had never seen before. Boris had once owned a car—a Stutz Bearcat, he claimed—but the condition of the streets had become too undependable for him, and he now did all his traveling on foot. Tucking the object that Victoria had given him under his arm, he would improvise routes as we walked along, always making certain to avoid the crowds. He would take me through back alleys and deserted paths, stepping neatly over the gutted pavement, navigating the numerous hazards and pitfalls, swerving now to his left, now to his right, not once breaking the rhythm of his step. He moved with surprising agility for a man of his girth, and I often had trouble keeping pace with him. Humming songs to himself, rattling on about one thing or another, Boris would dance along with nervous good humor as I trotted on behind. He seemed to know all the Resurrection Agents, and each one called forth a different routine from him: bursting through the door with open arms on some, slinking in quietly on others. Each personality had its vulnerable spot, and Boris always worked his pitch to the heart of it. If an agent had a weakness for flattery, Boris would flatter him; if an agent was fond of the color blue, Boris would give him something blue. Some had a preference for decorous behavior, others liked to play at being chums, still others were all business. Boris indulged them all, lying through his teeth without the slightest twinge of conscience. But that was part of the game, and not for a moment did Boris ever think it was not a game. His stories were preposterous, but he invented them so quickly, came up with such elaborate details, kept talking with an air of such conviction, that it was hard not to find yourself getting sucked in. "My dear good man," he would say, for example. "Take a careful look at this teacup. Hold it in your hand, if you wish. Close your eyes, put it to your lips, and imagine yourself drinking tea from it—just as I did thirty-one years ago, in the drawing rooms of Countess Oblomov. I was young back in those days, a student of literature at the university, and thin, if you can believe it, thin and handsome, with a beautiful head of curly hair. The Countess was the most ravishing woman in Minsk, a young widow of supernatural charms. The Count, scion of the great Oblomov fortune, had been killed in a duel—an affair of honor, which I need not discuss here—and you can imagine the effect this had on the men of her circle. Her suitors became legion; her salons were the envy of all Minsk. Such a woman, my friend, the image of her beauty has never left me: the brilliant red hair; the white, heaving bosom; the eyes flashing with wit—and yes, an ever-so-elusive hint of wickedness. It was enough to drive one mad. We vied with one another for her attention, we worshiped her, we wrote poetry to her, we were all deliriously in love. And yet it was I, the young Boris Stepanovich, it was I who succeeded in winning the favors of this singular temptress. I tell you this in all modesty. If you had been able to see me then, you would understand how this was possible. There were trysts in remote corners of the city, late-night meetings, secret visits to my garret (she would travel through the streets in disguise), and that long, rapturous summer I spent as a guest on her country estate. The Countess overwhelmed me with her generosity—not only of her person, which would have been enough, I assure you, more than enough!—but of the gifts she brought with her, the endless kindnesses she bestowed on me. A leather-bound set of Pushkin. A silver samovar. A gold watch. So many things, I could never list them all. Among them was an exquisite tea set that had once belonged to a member of the French court (the duc de Fântomas, I believe), which I used only when she came to visit me, hoarding it for those times when passion flung her across the snow-driven streets of Minsk and into my arms. Alas, time has been cruel. The set has suffered the fate of the years: saucers have cracked, cups have broken, a world has been lost. And yet, for all that, a single remnant has survived, a final link to the past. Treat it gently, my friend. You are holding my memories in your hand."

The trick, I think, was his ability to make inert things come to life. Boris Stepanovich steered the Resurrection men away from the objects themselves, coaxing them into a realm where the thing for sale was no longer the teacup but the Countess Oblomov herself. It didn't matter whether these stories were true or not. Once Boris's voice began working, it was enough to muddle the issue entirely. That voice was probably his greatest weapon. He possessed a superb range of modulations and timbres, and in his speeches he was always looping back and forth between hard sounds and soft, allowing the words to rise and fall as they poured out in a dense, intricately fashioned barrage of syllables. Boris had a weakness for hackneyed phrases and literary sentiments, but for all the deadness of the language, the stories were remarkably vivid. Delivery meant everything, and Boris did not hesitate to use even the lowest tricks. If necessary, he would cry real tears. If the situation called for it, he would smash an object on the floor. Once, to prove his faith in a set of fragile-looking glasses, he juggled them in the air for better than five minutes. I was always slightly embarrassed by these performances, but there was no question that they worked. Value is determined by supply and demand, after all, and the demand for precious antiques was hardly very great. Only the rich could afford them—the black market profiteers, the garbage brokers, the Resurrection Agents themselves—and it would have been wrong of Boris to insist on their utility. The whole point was that they were extravagances, things to possess because they functioned as symbols of wealth and power. Hence the stories about the Countess Oblomov and eighteenth-century French dukes. When you bought an antique vase from Boris Stepanovich, you were not just getting a vase, you were getting an entire world to go along with it.

Boris's apartment was in a small building on Turquoise Avenue, not more than ten minutes from Woburn House. After completing our business with the Resurrection Agents, we often went back there for a glass of tea. Boris was very fond of tea, and he usually served some kind of pastry to go along with it—scandalous treats from the House of Cakes on Windsor Boulevard: cream puffs, cinnamon buns, chocolate eclairs, all bought at horrific expense. Boris could not resist these minor indulgences, however, and he savored them slowly, his chewing accompanied by a faint musical rumbling in his throat, a steady undercurrent of sound that fell somewhere between laughter and a prolonged sigh. I took pleasure in these teas as well, but less for the food than for Boris's insistence on sharing it with me. My young widow friend is too wan, he would say. We must put more flesh on her bones, bring the bloom back to her cheeks, the bloom in the eyes of Miss Anna Blume herself. It was hard for me not to enjoy such treatment, and there were times when I sensed that all of Boris's ebullience was no more than a charade he performed for my benefit. One by one, he took on the roles of clown and scoundrel and philosopher, but the better I got to know him, the more I saw them as aspects of a single personality—marshaling its various weapons in an effort to bring me back to life. We became dear friends, and I owe Boris a debt for his compassion, for the devious and persistent attack he launched on the strongholds of my sadness.

The apartment was a shabby, three-room affair, cluttered with years of accumulation throughout—crockery, clothes, suitcases, blankets, rugs, every manner of bric-a-brac. Immediately upon returning home, Boris would withdraw to his bedroom and change out of his suit, carefully hanging it in the closet and then putting on a pair of old pants, slippers, and his bathrobe. This last item was a rather fantastical souvenir from the bygone days—a full-length concoction made of red velvet, with an ermine collar and cuffs, completely ragged by now, with mothholes in the sleeves and frayed material all along the back—but Boris wore it with his customary panache. After slicking back the strands of his thinning hair and dousing his neck with cologne, he would come striding out into the cramped and dusty living room to prepare the tea.

For the most part, he regaled me with stories of his life, but there were other times when we would look at various things in the room and talk about them—the boxes of curios, the bizarre little treasures, the detritus of a thousand buy-sell expeditions. Boris was particularly proud of his hat collection, which he stored in a large wooden trunk by the window. I don't know how many he had in there, but two or three dozen I would think, perhaps more. Sometimes, he would pick out a couple of them for us to wear while we were having our tea. This game amused him very much, and I admit that I enjoyed it myself, although I would be hard-pressed to explain why. There were cowboy hats and derbies, fezes and pith helmets, mortarboards and berets—every kind of headgear you could imagine. Whenever I asked Boris why he collected them, he would give me a different answer. Once, he said that wearing hats was part of his religion. Another time, he explained that each of his hats had once belonged to a relative and that he wore them in order to commune with the souls of his dead ancestors. By putting on a hat, he acquired the spiritual qualities of its former owner, he said. True enough, he had given each of his hats a name, but I took those more as projections of his private feelings about the hats than as representing people who had actually lived. The fez, for example, was Uncle Abduhl. The derby was Sir Charles. The mortarboard was Professor Solomon. On still another occasion, however,

153

when I brought up the subject again, Boris explained that he liked to wear hats because they kept his thoughts from flying out of his head. If we both wore them while we drank our tea, then we were bound to have more intelligent and stimulating conversations. "*Le chapeau influence le cerveau*," he said, lapsing into French. "*Si on protège la tête, la pensée n'est plus bête.*"

There was only one time when Boris ever seemed to let his guard down, and that was the talk I remember best, the one that stands out most vividly for me now. It was raining that afternoon—a dreary, all-day soak—and I dawdled longer than usual, reluctant to leave the warmth of the apartment and go back to Woburn House. Boris was in an oddly pensive mood, and for the better part of the visit I had done most of the talking. Just when I finally mustered the courage to put on my coat and say good-bye (I remember the smell of damp wool, the reflections of the candles in the window, the cavelike interiority of the moment), Boris reached out for my hand and held it tightly in his own, looking up at me with a grim, enigmatic smile.

"You must understand that it's all an illusion, my dear," he said.

"I'm not sure I know what you mean, Boris."

"Woburn House. It's built on a foundation of clouds."

"It seems perfectly solid to me. I'm there every day, you know, and the house has never moved. It hasn't even wobbled."

"For now, yes. But give it a little time, and then you'll see what I'm talking about."

"How much time is 'a little time'?"

"However long it takes. The fifth-floor rooms can hold

154

only so much, you understand, and sooner or later there won't be anything left to sell. The stock is growing thin already—and once a thing is gone, there's no getting it back."

"Is that so terrible? Everything ends, Boris. I don't see why Woburn House should be any different."

"It's fine for you to say that. But what about poor Victoria?"

"Victoria isn't stupid. I'm sure she's thought about these things herself."

"Victoria is also stubborn. She'll hold out until the last glot has been spent, and then she'll be no better off than the people she's been trying to help."

"Isn't that her business?"

"Yes and no. I promised her father that I would look after her, and I'm not about to break my word. If only you could have seen her when she was young—years ago, before the collapse. So beautiful, so filled with life. It torments me to think that anything bad could happen to her."

"I'm surprised at you, Boris. You sound like a rank sentimentalist."

"We all speak our own language of ghosts, I'm afraid. I've read the handwriting on the wall, and none of it encourages me. The Woburn House funds will run out. I have additional resources in this apartment, of course"—and here Boris made a sweeping gesture that took in all the objects in the room—"but these too will be quickly exhausted. Unless we begin to look ahead, there won't be much future for any of us."

"What are you trying to say?"

"Make plans. Consider the possibilities. Act."

"And you expect Victoria to go along with you?"

"Not necessarily. But if I have you on my side, at least there's a chance."

"What makes you think I could have any influence on her?"

"The eyes in my head. I see what's going on over there, Anna. Victoria has never responded to anyone the way she has to you. She's positively smitten."

"We're just friends."

"There's more to it than that, my dear. A great deal more."

"I don't know what you're talking about."

"You will. Sooner or later, you'll understand every word I've said. I guarantee it."

Boris was right. Eventually, I did understand. Eventually, all the things that were on the brink of happening did happen. It took me a long time to catch on, however. In fact, I did not really see them until they hit me in the face— but that is perhaps excusable, given that I am the most ignorant person who ever lived.

Bear with me. I know that I am beginning to stammer here, but words do not come readily for saying what I want to say. You must try to imagine how things were for us back then—the sense of doom weighing down on us, the air of unreality that seemed to hover around each moment. Lesbianism is only a clinical term, and it does not do justice to the facts. Victoria and I did not become a couple in the usual sense of the word. Rather, we each became a refuge for the other, the place where each of us could go to find comfort in her solitude. In the long run, the sex was the least important part of it. A body is just a body, after all, and it hardly seems to matter whether the hand that is touching you belongs to a man or a woman. Being with Victoria gave me pleasure, but it also gave me the courage to live in the present again. That was the thing that counted most. I no longer looked back all the time, and little by little this seemed to repair some of the innumerable hurts I carried around inside me. I was not made whole again, but at least I did not hate my life anymore. A woman had fallen in love with me, and then I discovered that I was able to love her. I am not asking you to understand this, merely to accept it as a fact. There are many things in my life that I regret, but this is not one of them.

It started toward the end of summer, three or four months after I arrived at Woburn House. Victoria came into my room for one of our late-night talks, and I remember that I was dog-tired, aching in the small of my back and feeling even more despondent than usual. She began rubbing my back in a friendly sort of way, trying to relax my muscles, doing the same kind and sisterly thing that anyone would do under those circumstances. No one had touched me in months, however—not since the last night I had spent with Sam—and I had almost forgotten how good it feels to be massaged like that. Victoria kept moving her hands up and down my spine, and eventually she slipped them under my T-shirt, putting her fingers on my bare skin. It was extraordinary to have that done to me, and soon I began to float from the pleasure of it, feeling as though my body was about to come apart. Even then, however, I don't think that either one of us knew what was going to happen. It was a slow process, and it meandered from stage to stage with no clear object in mind. At some point the sheet slipped off my legs, and I did not bother to retrieve it. Victoria's hands swept over more and more of me, taking in my legs and buttocks, roaming down my flanks and up along my shoulders, and at last there was no place on my body I did not want her to touch. I rolled onto my back, and there was Victoria leaning over me, naked under her bathrobe, with one breast hanging out of the parted opening. You're so beautiful, I said to her, I think I want to die. I sat up slightly and began to kiss that breast, that round and beautiful breast that was so much larger than mine, kissing the soft brown aureole, moving my tongue along the crosshatch of blue veins that stood just below the surface. It felt like a grave and shocking thing to me, and for the first moment or two I sensed that I had stumbled onto a desire that could be found only in the darkness of dreams—but that feeling did not last very long, and afterward I let myself go, was carried away by it completely.

We continued to sleep together for the next few months, and finally I began to feel at home there. The nature of the work at Woburn House was too demoralizing without someone to count on, without some permanent place in which to anchor your feelings. Too many people came and went, too many lives shuttled past you, and by the time you got to know someone, he was already packing up his things and moving on. Then someone else would come, sleeping in the bed once occupied by the other, sitting in the same chair, walking over the same patch of ground, and then the time would come for that person to leave, and the process would be repeated again. As opposed to all this, Victoria and I were there for each other—through thick and thin, as we used to say—and that was the one thing that did not change, in spite of the changes occurring around us. Because of this bond, I was able to reconcile myself to the work, and that in turn had a calming effect on my spirits. Then more things happened, and it was no longer possible for us to go on as we had. I will speak of this in a moment, but the important thing was that nothing really changed. The bond was still there, and once and for all I learned what a remarkable person Victoria was.

It was the middle of December, just around the time of the first serious cold spell. The winter did not turn out to be as brutal as the one before it, but no one could have known that in advance. The cold brought back all the bad memories of the previous year, and you could feel the panic mounting in the streets, the desperation of the people as they tried to brace themselves for the onslaught. The lines outside Woburn House became longer than at any time in the past several months, and I found myself working extra hours just to keep pace with the flow. On the morning I am talking about, I remember seeing ten or eleven people in rapid succession, each with his own gruesome story to tell. One of them—Melissa Reilly was her name, a woman of about sixty—was so distraught that she broke down and cried in front of me, clutching my hand and asking me to help her find her lost husband, who had wandered off in June and hadn't been heard from since. What do you expect me to do? I said. I can't leave my post and go off traipsing through the streets with you, there's too much work to be done here. She kept on making a scene, however, and I found myself getting angry at her for being so insistent. Look, I said, you're not the only woman in this city who's lost a husband. Mine has been gone just as long as yours, and for all I know he's just as dead as yours is, too. Do you see me crying and pulling my hair out? It's something we all have to face. I loathed myself for spouting such platitudes, for dealing with her so brusquely, but she was making it hard for me to think with all her hysterics and incoherent babbling about Mr. Reilly and their children and the honeymoon trip they had taken thirty-seven years ago. I don't care about you, she finally said to me. A cold-hearted bitch like you doesn't deserve to have a husband, and you can take your fancy Woburn House and stick it between your eyes. If the good doctor could hear you talk, he'd be turning over in his grave. Something like that, although I can't remember her exact words. Then Mrs. Reilly rose to her feet and departed in a last huff of indignation. The moment she was gone, I lay my head down on the desk and shut my eyes, wondering if I was not too exhausted to see any more people that day. The interview had been a disaster, and it had been my fault for letting my feelings run away from me. There was no excuse for that, no justification for venting my troubles on a poor woman who was obviously half out of her mind with grief. I must have dozed off just then, perhaps for five minutes, perhaps for only an instant or two—I can't say for sure. All I know is that an infinite distance seemed to lie between that moment and the next, between the moment when I closed my eyes and opened them again. I looked up, and there was Sam, sitting in the chair across from me for the next interview. At first I thought I was still asleep. He's a figment, I said to myself. He comes from one of those dreams in which you imagine yourself waking up, but the waking is only part of the dream. Then I said to myself: Sam— and immediately understood that it could be no one else. This was Sam, but it was also not Sam. This was Sam in another body, with graying hair and bruises on the side of his face, with black, torn-up fingers and devastated clothes.

He sat there with a dead, wholly absent look in his eyes—drifting inside himself, it seemed to me, utterly lost. I saw everything in a rush, a whirlwind, a flicker. This was Sam, but he did not recognize me, he did not know who I was. I felt my heart pound, and for a moment I thought I was going to faint. Then, very slowly, two tears began to fall down Sam's cheeks. He was biting his lower lip, and his chin was trembling out of control. Suddenly, his whole body started to shake, air spurted from his mouth, and the sob he was struggling to keep inside him shuddered out. He turned his face away from me, still trying to keep himself in check, but the spasms kept jolting his body, and the breathless, rasping noise kept escaping from his shut lips. I stood up from my chair, staggered to the other side of the desk, and put my arms around him. The moment I touched him, I heard the sound of crumpled newspapers rustling in his coat. A moment after that, I began to cry, and then I couldn't stop. I held on to him as hard as I could, digging my face down into the material of his coat, and couldn't find a way to stop.

That was more than a year ago. Weeks went by before Sam was well enough to talk about the things that had happened to him, but even then his stories were vague, filled with inconsistencies and blanks. It all seemed to run together, he said, and he had trouble distinguishing the outlines of events, could not disentangle one day from another. He remembered waiting for me to show up, sitting in the room until six or seven the next morning, and then finally going out to look for me. It was after midnight when he returned, and by then the library was already in flames. He stood among the crowds of people who had gathered to watch the fire, and then, as the roof finally collapsed, saw our book burn up along with everything else in the building. He said that he could actually see it in his mind, that he actually knew the precise moment when the flames entered our room and ate up the pages of the manuscript.

After that, everything lost definition for him. He had the money in his pocket, the clothes on his back, and that was all. For two months he did little else but look for me—sleeping wherever he could, eating only when he had no choice. In this way he managed to keep himself afloat, but by the end of the summer his money was nearly gone. Worse than that, he said, he finally gave up looking for me. He was convinced that I was dead, and he could no longer bear to torture himself with false hope. He withdrew to a corner of Diogenes Terminal—the old train station in the northwest part of the city—and lived among the derelicts and madmen, the shadow people who wandered through the long corridors and abandoned waiting rooms. It was like turning into an animal, he said, an underground creature who had gone into hibernation. Once or twice a week, he would hire himself out to carry heavy loads for scavengers, working for the pittance they gave him, but for the most part he did nothing, refusing to stir himself unless absolutely compelled to. "I gave up trying to be anyone," he said. "The object of my life was to remove myself from my surroundings, to live in a place where nothing could hurt me anymore. One by one, I tried to abandon my attachments, to let go of all the things I ever cared about. The idea was to achieve indifference, an indifference so powerful and sublime that it would protect me from further assault. I said good-bye to you, Anna; I said good-bye

162

to the book; I said good-bye to the thought of going home. I even tried to say good-bye to myself. Little by little, I became as serene as a Buddha, sitting in my corner and paying no attention to the world around me. If it hadn't been for my body—the occasional demands of my stomach, my bowels—I might never have moved again. To want nothing, I kept saying to myself, to have nothing, to be nothing. I could imagine no more perfect solution than that. In the end, I came close to living the life of a stone."

We gave Sam the room on the second floor that I had once lived in. He was in dreadful condition, and for the first ten days it was touch and go at best. I spent nearly all my time with him, skimping on my other duties as much as possible, and Victoria did not object. That was what I found so remarkable about her. Not only did she not object, but she went out of her way to encourage it. There was something supernatural about her understanding of the situation, her ability to absorb the sudden, almost violent end to the way we had been living. I kept expecting her to force a showdown, to erupt in some display of disappointment or jealousy, but nothing of the sort ever occurred. Her first response to the news was happiness—happiness for my sake, happiness for the fact that Sam was alive—and afterward she worked as hard as I did to see that he recovered. She had suffered a private loss, but she also knew that his being there represented a gain for Woburn House. The thought of having another man on the staff, especially one like Sam—who was neither old like Frick nor slow-witted and inexperienced like Willie—was enough to square the ledger for her. This single-mindedness could be rather frightening, I found, but nothing was more important to Victoria than Woburn House—not even me, not even herself, if such a thing can be imagined. I don't want to be overly simplistic, but as time went on I almost began to feel that she had allowed me to fall in love with her so that I would be able to get well. Now that I was better, she shifted the focus of her attention to Sam. Woburn House was her only reality you see, and in the end there was nothing that did not give way to it.

Eventually, Sam came upstairs to live with me on the fourth floor. He slowly put on weight, slowly began to resemble the person he had once been, but not everything could be the same for him—not now, not anymore. I am not just talking about the ordeals his body had been through—the prematurely gray hair, the missing teeth, the slight but persistent trembling in his hands—I am talking about inner things as well. Sam was no longer the arrogant young man I had lived with in the library. He had been changed by his experiences, humbled by them almost, and there was a softer, more placid rhythm to his manner now. He talked periodically of starting the book again, but I could see that his heart wasn't in it. The book was no longer a solution for him, and once that fixation was lost, he seemed better able to understand the things that had happened to him, that were happening to all of us. His strength returned, and little by little we got used to each other again, but it seemed to me that we stood on more equal terms than we had before. Perhaps I had changed during those months as well, but the fact was that I sensed that Sam needed me more than he had back then, and I liked that sense of being needed so much, I liked it better than anything else in the world.

He started working around the beginning of February. At first, I was totally against the job that Victoria had devised for him. She had given the matter a great deal of thought, she said, and in the end she believed that Sam could best serve the interests of Woburn House by becoming the new doctor. "You might find this a strange idea," she continued, "but ever since my father's death, we've been floundering. There's no cohesion to the place anymore, no sense of purpose. We give people food and shelter for a little while, and that's all—a minimal kind of sustenance that barely helps anyone. In the old days, people would come because they wanted to be near my father. Even when he couldn't help them as a doctor, he was there to talk to them and listen to their troubles. That was the important thing. He made people feel better just by being who he was. People were given food, but they were also given hope. If we had another doctor around here now, maybe we could get closer to the spirit this place once had."

"But Sam isn't a doctor," I said. "It would be a lie, and I don't see how you can help people if the first thing you do is lie to them."

"This isn't lying," Victoria answered. "It's a masquerade. You tell lies for selfish reasons, but in this case we wouldn't be taking anything for ourselves. It's for other people, a way of giving them hope. As long as they think that Sam is a doctor, they'll believe in what he says."

"But what if someone finds out? We'd be finished then. No one would trust us after that—not even when we told the truth."

"No one will find out. Sam can't give himself away, because he won't be practicing medicine. Even if he wanted to, there's no medicine left for him to practice with. We have a couple of bottles of aspirin, a box or two of bandages, and that's about it. Just because he calls himself Dr. Farr, that doesn't mean he'll be doing what a doctor does. He'll talk, and people will listen to him. That's all it amounts to. A way of giving people a chance to find their own strength."

"What if Sam can't pull it off?"

"Then he can't. But we won't know that unless he tries, will we?"

In the end, Sam agreed to go along with it. "It's not something I would have thought of myself," he said, "not if I lived for another hundred years. Anna finds it cynical, and in the long run I think she's right. But who knows if the facts aren't just as cynical? People are dying out there, and whether we give them a bowl of soup or save their souls, they're still going to die. I don't see any way of getting around that. If Victoria thinks that having a fake doctor to talk to will make things easier for them, who am I to say she's wrong? I doubt it will do much good, but there doesn't seem to be much harm in it either. It's an attempt at something, and I'm willing to go along with it for that."

I didn't blame Sam for saying yes, but I continued to be angry with Victoria for some time. It had shocked me to see her justifying her fanaticism with such elaborate arguments about right and wrong. Whatever you wanted to call it—a lie, a masquerade, a means to an end—this plan struck me as a betrayal of her father's principles. I had had enough qualms about Woburn House already, and if anything had helped me to accept the place at all, it was Victoria herself. Her straightforwardness, the clarity of her motives, the moral rigor I had found in her—these things had been an example to me, and they had given me the strength to go on. Now, suddenly, there seemed to be a realm of darkness in her that I had not noticed before. It was a disillusionment, I think, and for a time I actually resented her, was appalled that she should turn out to be so like everyone else. But then, as I began to understand the situation more clearly, my anger passed. Victoria had managed to hide the truth from me, but the fact was that Woburn House was on the verge of going under. The masquerade with Sam was no more than an attempt to salvage something from the disaster, an eccentric little coda tacked on to a piece that was already played out. Everything was finished. It was just that I didn't know it yet.

The irony was that Sam was a success in his role as doctor. All the props were there for him—the white coat, the black bag, the stethoscope, the thermometer—and he used them to full effect. There was no question that he looked like a doctor, but after a while he began to act like one, too. That was the incredible part of it. At first, I was rather grudging about this transformation, not wanting to admit that Victoria had been right; but eventually I had to give in to the facts. People responded to Sam. He had a way of listening to them that made them want to talk, and words came flooding from their mouths the moment he sat down to be with them. His training as a journalist no doubt helped in all this, but now he had been imbued with an added measure of dignity, a persona of benevolence, as it were, and because people trusted that persona, they told him things he had never heard from anyone before. It was like being a confessor, he said, and little by little he began to appreciate the good that comes when people are allowed to unburden themselves—the salutary effect of speaking words, of releasing words that tell the story of what happened to them. The temptation would have been to start believing in the role, I think, but Sam managed to keep his distance from it. He joked about it in private, and eventually he came up with a new set of names for himself—Doctor Shamuel Farr, Doctor Quackingsham, Doctor Bunk. Underneath this jocularity, however, I sensed that the job meant more to him than he was willing to admit. His pose as doctor had suddenly given him access to the intimate thoughts of others, and these thoughts now became a part of who he was. His interior world grew larger, sturdier, more able to absorb the things that were put into it. "It's better not having to be myself," he once told me. "If I didn't have that other person to hide behind—the one who wears the white coat and the sympathetic look on his face—I don't think I could stand it. The stories would crush me. As it is, I have a way to listen to them now, to put them where they belong—next to my own story, next to the story of the self I no longer have to be as long as I am listening to them."

Spring came early that year, and by mid-March the crocuses were flowering in the garden out back—yellow and purple stalks jutting from the grassy margins, the burgeoning green mixed with pools of drying mud. Even the nights were warm then, and sometimes Sam and I would take a short walk around the enclosure before turning in. It was good to be out there for those few moments, with the windows of the house dark behind us, and the stars burning faintly overhead. Each time we took one of those little walks, I felt that I was falling in love with him all over again, each time falling for him in that darkness, hanging on to his arm and remembering how it had been for us in the beginning, back in the days of the Terrible Winter, when we lived in the library and looked out every night

168

through the big, fan-shaped window. We didn't talk about the future anymore. We didn't make plans or talk about going home. The present consumed us entirely now, and with all the work to be done every day, with all the exhaustion that followed from it, there was no time to think about anything else. There was a ghostly equilibrium to this life, but that did not necessarily make it bad, and at times I almost found myself happy to be living it, to be going along with things as they were.

Those things could not continue, of course. They were an illusion, just as Boris Stepanovich had said they were, and nothing could stop the changes from coming. By the end of April, we began to feel the pinch. Victoria finally broke down and explained the situation to us, and then, one by one, the necessary economies were made. The Wednesday afternoon rounds went first. There was no point in spending money on the car, we decided. The fuel was too expensive, and there were enough people waiting for us right outside the door. No need to go out looking for them, Victoria said, and not even Frick raised an objection to that. That same afternoon, we went for a last spin through the city—Frick at the wheel with Willie beside him, Sam and I in back. We chugged along the peripheral boulevards, dipped in occasionally for a look at this neighborhood or that, felt the bumps as Frick maneuvered the car over the ruts and potholes. None of us said much of anything. We just watched the sights as they slid past us, a bit awed that this would never happen again, I think, that this was the last time, and soon it was as though we were not even looking anymore, just sitting in our seats and feeling the odd despair of driving around in circles. Afterward, Frick put the car in the garage and locked the door, and from then on I don't think he ever opened it again. Once, when we were out in the garden together, he pointed to the garage across the way, and broke into a broad, toothless smile. "Them things what you see when nothing more," he said. "Say good-bye and then forget. A shining in the head now. Whoosh it goes, you see, and gone. All aglow and then forget."

The clothes went next—all the free handouts we had given to the residents, the shirts and shoes, the jackets and sweaters, the trousers, the hats, the old pairs of gloves. Boris Stepanovich had bought these things in bulk from a supplier in the fourth census zone, but that man was out of business now, had in fact been run out of it by a consortium of thugs and Resurrection Agents, and we no longer had the means to keep this end of the operation going. Even in good times the purchase of clothes had accounted for thirty to forty percent of the Woburn House budget. Now, when hard times had finally come, we had no choice but to strike this expense from the books. No cutbacks, no gradual diminishments—the whole thing all at once, axed in one go. Victoria started a campaign of what she called "conscientious mending," stocking up on various kinds of sewing equipment—needles, spools of thread, cloth patches, thimbles, darning eggs, and so on—and did what she could to restore the clothes that people already had when they arrived at Woburn House. The idea was to spare as much money as possible for food, and given that this was the most important thing, the thing that did the most good for the residents, we all agreed on the correctness of this approach. Still, as the fifth-floor rooms continued to empty out, not even the food supply could withstand the erosion. One by one, items were eliminated—sugar, salt, butter, fruit, the small rations of meat we had allowed ourselves, the occasional glass of milk. Each time Victoria announced another one of these economies, Maggie Vine would throw a fit—erupting into a wild clown's pantomime of a person in tears, banging her head against the wall, flapping her arms against her legs as though she meant to fly away. It was no picnic for any of us, however. We had all grown accustomed to having enough to eat, and these deprivations caused a painful shock to our systems. I had to think through the whole question for myself again—what it means to be hungry, how to detach the idea of food from the idea of pleasure, how to accept what you are given and not crave for more. By mid-summer our diet was down to a variety of grains, starches, and root vegetables—turnips, beets, carrots. We tried to plant a garden out back, but seeds were scarce, and we managed to grow only a few heads of lettuce. Maggie improvised as best she could, boiling up a number of thin soups, angrily preparing concoctions of beans and noodles, pounding out dumplings in a swirl of white flour—gooey dough balls that nearly made one gag. Compared to how we had been eating before, this was awful stuff, but it kept us alive for all that. The grim thing was not really the quality of the food, but the certainty that things were only going to get worse. Little by little, the distinction between Woburn House and the rest of the city was growing smaller. We were being swallowed up, and not one of us knew how to prevent it.

Then Maggie disappeared. One day she simply wasn't there anymore, and we found no clues to tell us where she had gone. She must have wandered off while the rest of us were asleep upstairs, but that hardly explained why she had left all her things behind. If she had meant to run away, it seemed logical to think she would have packed a bag for the journey. Willie spent two or three days searching the immediate area for her, but he couldn't find a trace, and none of the people he talked to had ever seen her. After that, Willie and I took over the kitchen duties. Just as we were beginning to feel comfortable with the work, however, something else happened. Suddenly, and without any warning at all, Willie's grandfather died. We tried to comfort ourselves with the thought that Frick had been old—almost eighty, Victoria said—but that didn't do much good. He died in his sleep one night in early October, and Willie was the one who discovered the body: waking up in the morning and seeing that his grandfather was still in bed, and then, when he tried to rouse him, watching in horror as the old man crashed to the floor. It was hardest on Willie, of course, but we all suffered from this death in our own ways. Sam wept bitter tears when it happened, and Boris Stepanovich did not speak to anyone for four hours after he was told the news, which must have been some kind of record for him. Victoria did not show much on the surface, but then she went ahead and did something rash, and I understood how close she was to an ultimate despair. It is absolutely against the law to bury the dead. All corpses are required to be taken to one of the Transformation Centers, and anyone who does not comply with this regulation is subject to the stiffest penalty: a fine of two hundred fifty glots, to be paid on issuance of the summons, or immediate exile to one of the work camps in the southwestern part of the country. In spite of all that, within an hour of learning of Frick's death, Victoria announced that she was planning to hold a funeral for him in the garden that afternoon. Sam tried to talk her out of it, but she refused to budge. "No one will ever know," she said. "And even if the police do find out, it doesn't matter. We have to do what's right. If we let a stupid law stand in our way, then we aren't worth anything." It was a reckless, wholly irresponsible act, but at bottom I believe she was doing it for Willie's sake. Willie was a boy of less than normal intelligence, and at seventeen he was still locked into the violence of a self that understood almost nothing of the world around him. Frick had taken care of him, had done his thinking for him, had literally walked him through the paces of his life. With his grandfather suddenly gone, there was no telling what might happen to him. Willie needed a gesture from us now—a clear and dramatic assertion of our loyalty, proof that we would stand with him no matter what the consequences. The burial was an enormous risk, but even in the light of what happened, I don't think Victoria was wrong to take it.

Before the ceremony, Willie went into the garage, unscrewed the horn from the car, and spent the better part of an hour polishing it up. It was one of those old-fashioned horns you used to see on children's bicycles—but larger and more impressive, with a brass trumpet and a black rubber knob almost the size of a grapefruit. Then he and Sam dug a hole next to the hawthorn bushes out back. Six of the residents carried Frick's body from the house to the grave, and as they lowered him into the ground, Willie put the horn on his grandfather's chest, making sure that it was buried along with him. Boris Stepanovich then read a short poem he had written for the occasion, and afterward Sam and Willie shoveled the dirt back into the hole. It was a primitive ceremony at best—no prayers, no songs— but just to be doing it was significant enough. Everyone

173

was out there together—all the residents, all the members of the staff—and by the time it was over, most of us had tears in our eyes. A small stone was placed on the gravesite to mark the spot, and then we went back into the house.

Afterward, we all tried to pick up the slack as far as Willie was concerned. Victoria delegated new responsibilities to him, even allowing him to stand guard with the rifle while I was conducting interviews in the hall, and Sam made an effort to take him under his wing—teaching the boy how to shave properly, how to write his name in longhand, how to add and subtract. Willie responded well to this attention. If not for a dismal stroke of luck, I believe he would have come around quite nicely. About two weeks after Frick's funeral, however, a policeman from the Central Constabulary paid us a visit. He was a ridiculous-looking character, all pudgy and red-faced, sporting one of the new uniforms that had recently been given to officers from that branch of the service—a bright red tunic, white jodhpurs, and black, patent leather boots with kepi to match. He fairly creaked in this absurd costume, and because he insisted on thrusting out his chest, I actually thought he might pop his buttons. He clicked his heels and saluted when I answered the door, and if it hadn't been for the machine gun slung over his shoulder, I probably would have told him to leave. "Is this the residence of Victoria Woburn?" he said. "Yes," I said. "Among others." "Then step aside, Miss," he answered, pushing me out of the way and entering the hall. "The investigation is about to begin."

I will spare you the details. The upshot was that someone had reported the funeral to the police, and they had come to verify the complaint. It had to have been one of the residents, but this was an act of such astonishing betrayal

174

that none of us had the heart to try to figure out who it was. Someone who had been present at the funeral no doubt, who had been forced to leave Woburn House after his allotted stay and bore a grudge for being driven back into the streets. That was a logical guess, but it didn't much matter anymore. Perhaps the police had paid this person money, perhaps he had merely done it out of spite. Whatever the case, the information was deadly accurate. The constable strode out into the back garden with two assistants trailing behind him, scanned the enclosure for several moments, and then pointed right to the spot where the grave had been dug. Shovels were ordered, and the two assistants promptly fell to work, searching for the corpse they already knew was there. "This is most irregular," the constable said. "The selfishness of burial in this day and age—imagine the gall of it. Without bodies to burn, we'd go under fast, that's for sure, the whole lot of us would be sunk. Where would our fuel come from, how would we keep ourselves alive? In this time of national emergency, we must all be vigilant. Not one body can be spared, and those who take it upon themselves to subvert this law must not be allowed to go free. They are evildoers of the worst sort, perfidious malefactors, renegade scum. They must be rooted out and punished."

We were all out in the garden by then, crowding around the grave as this fool prattled on with his vicious, empty-headed remarks. Victoria's face had gone white, and if I hadn't been there to prop her up, I think she might have collapsed. On the other side of the expanding hole, Sam was keeping a careful watch over Willie. The boy was in tears, and as the constable's assistants continued to shovel up the earth and fling it carelessly into the bushes, he began

175

to cry out in a panic-stricken voice, "That's grandpa's dirt. You shouldn't be throwing it away. That dirt belongs to grandpa." It got so loud that the constable had to stop in the middle of his harangue. He eyed Willie with contempt, and then, just as he began to move his arm in the direction of his machine gun, Sam clapped his hand over Willie's mouth and began to drag him off toward the house—struggling to keep him in check as the boy squirmed and kicked his way across the lawn. In the meantime, a number of the residents had fallen to the ground and were begging the constable to believe in their innocence. They knew nothing of this heinous crime; they had not been there when it happened; if anyone had told them of such foul doings, they never would have agreed to stay there; they were all being held prisoner against their will. One cringing statement after another, an outbreak of mass cowardice. I felt so disgusted I wanted to spit. One old woman—Beulah Stansky was her name—actually grabbed hold of the constable's boot and began to kiss it. He tried to shrug her off, but when she wouldn't let go, he drove the tip of his boot into her belly and sent her sprawling—moaning and whimpering like a beaten dog. Fortunately for all of us, Boris Stepanovich chose to make his entrance at precisely this moment. He opened the French windows at the back of the house, gingerly stepped out onto the lawn, and strolled over to the hubbub with a calm, almost bemused look on his face. It was as though he had witnessed this scene a hundred times before, and nothing was going to ruffle him—not the police, not the guns, not one bit of it. They were pulling the body out of the hole when he joined us, and there was poor Frick stretched out on the grass, the eyes now gone from his head, face all smeared with dirt, and a

176

horde of white worms writhing in his mouth. Boris did not even bother to glance at him. He walked straight up to the constable in the red coat, addressed him as general, and then proceeded to draw him off to the side. I did not hear what they said, but I could see that Boris hardly stopped grinning and twitching his eyebrows as they talked. Eventually, a wad of cash emerged from his pocket, he peeled off one bill after another from the roll, and then placed the money in the constable's hand. I didn't know what this meant—whether Boris had paid the fine or whether they had struck some sort of private agreement—but that was the extent of the transaction: a short, swift exchange of cash, and then the business was done. The assistants carried Frick's body across the lawn, through the house, and then out to the front, where they tossed it into the back of a truck that was parked in the street. The constable harangued us once more on the steps—very sternly, using the same words he had used in the garden—and then gave a final salute, clicked his heels, and walked down to the truck, shooing aside the bedraggled onlookers with short flicks of his hand. As soon as he had driven off with his men, I ran back out into the garden to look for the car horn. I thought I would polish it up again and give it to Willie, but I couldn't find it. I even climbed down into the open grave to see if it was there, but it wasn't. Like so many other things before it, the horn had vanished without a trace.

Our necks were saved for a little while. No one would be going to prison, in any event, but the money that Boris forked over to the constable had pretty much exhausted our reserves. Within three days of Frick's exhumation, the last items from the fifth floor were sold off: a gold-plated letter opener, a mahogany end table, and the blue velvet curtains that had hung on the windows. After that, we scraped up some additional cash by selling books from the downstairs library—two shelves of Dickens, five sets of Shakespeare (one of them in thirty-eight miniature volumes no bigger than the palm of your hand), a Jane Austen, a Schopenhauer, an illustrated *Don Quixote*—but the bottom had fallen out of the book market by then, and these things fetched no more than a trifle. From that point on, it was Boris who carried us. His store of objects was far from infinite, however, and we did not delude ourselves into thinking it would last for very long. We gave ourselves three or four months at best. With winter coming on again, we knew it would probably be less than that.

The sensible thing would have been to shut down Woburn House right then. We tried to talk Victoria into it, but it was hard for her to take that step, and several weeks of uncertainty followed. Then, just as Boris seemed on the point of convincing her, the decision was taken out of her hands, was taken out of all our hands. I am referring to Willie. With hindsight, it seems perfectly inevitable that it should have worked out that way, but I would be lying to you if I said that any of us could see it coming. We were all too involved in the tasks at hand, and when the thing finally happened, it was like a bolt from the blue, like an explosion from the depths of the earth.

After Frick's body was carried off, Willie was never really the same. He continued to do his work, but only in silence, in a solitude of blank stares and shrugs. As soon as you got close to him, his eyes would blaze with hostility and resentment, and once he even threw my hand off his shoulder as though he meant to hurt me if I ever did it again. Working together as we did in the kitchen every day, I probably spent more time with him than anyone else. I did my best to help, but I don't think anything I said ever got through to him. Your grandfather is all right, Willie, I would say. He's in heaven now, and what happens to his body is unimportant. His soul is alive, and he wouldn't want you to be worrying about him like this. Nothing can hurt him. He's happy where he is now, and he wants you to be happy, too. I felt like a parent trying to explain death to a small child, mouthing the same hypocritical nonsense I had heard from my own parents. It didn't matter what I said, however, for Willie wasn't buying any of it. He was a prehistoric man, and the only way he could respond to death was to worship his departed ancestor, to think of him as a god. Victoria had instinctively understood this. Frick's burial site had become holy ground for Willie, and now it had been desecrated. The order of things had been smashed, and no amount of talk from me would ever set it right.

He began going out after dinner, rarely returning before two or three in the morning. It was impossible to know what he did out there in the streets, since he never talked about it, and there was no point in asking him any questions. One morning he failed to show up altogether. I thought that perhaps he was gone for good, but then, just after lunch, he walked into the kitchen without a word and started chopping vegetables, almost daring me to be impressed by his arrogance. It was late November by then, and Willie had spun off into his own orbit, an errant star with no definable trajectory. I gave up depending on him to do his share of the work. When he was there, I accepted his help; when he was gone, I did the work myself. Once, he stayed away for two days before coming back; another time it was three days. These gradually lengthening absences lulled us into thinking that he was somehow fading away from us. Sooner or later, we thought, a time would come when he wouldn't be there anymore, more or less in the same way that Maggie Vine wasn't there anymore. There was so much for us to do just then, the scramble to keep our sinking ship afloat was so exhausting, that one tended not to think about Willie when he wasn't around. He stayed away for six days the next time, and at that point I think we all felt that we had seen the last of him. Then, very late one night during the first week of December, we were startled awake by a horrendous thumping and crashing from the downstairs rooms. My initial reaction was to think that people from the line outside had broken into the house, but then, just as Sam sprang out of bed and grabbed the shotgun we kept in our room, there was a sound of machine gun fire down below, a huge burst and splatter of bullets, and then more and more of it. I heard people screaming, felt the house shake with footsteps, heard the machine gun go tearing into the walls, the windows, the splintering floors. I lit a candle and followed Sam to the head of the stairs, fully expecting to see the constable or one of his men, girding myself for the moment when I would be shot to pieces. Victoria was already racing down ahead of us, and from what I could gather she was unarmed. It wasn't the constable, of course, though I don't doubt that it was his gun. Willie was on the second-floor landing, making his way up to us with the weapon in his hands. My candle was too far off for me to get a look at his face, but I saw him pause when he noticed that Victoria was coming toward him.

"That's enough, Willie," she said. "Drop the gun. Drop the gun right now." I don't know if he was planning to fire at her, but the fact was that he did not drop it. Sam was standing next to Victoria by then, and an instant after she spoke those words, he pulled the trigger of his shotgun. The blast hit Willie in the chest, and suddenly he was flying backward, tumbling down the stairs until he reached the bottom. He was dead before he got there, I think, dead before he even knew he had been shot.

That was six or seven weeks ago. Of the eighteen residents who were living here at the time, seven were killed, five managed to escape, three were wounded, and three were unhurt. Mr. Hsia, a newcomer who had performed card tricks for us the night before, died from his bullet wounds at eleven o'clock the next morning. Mr. Rosenberg and Mrs. Rudniki both recovered. We took care of them for more than a week, and once they were strong enough to walk again, we sent them away. They were the last residents of Woburn House. The morning after the disaster, Sam made a sign and hammered it onto the front door: WOBURN HOUSE CLOSED. The people outside did not go away immediately, but then it got very cold, and as the days went by and the door did not open, the crowds began to disperse. Since then, we have been sitting tight, making plans about what to do next, trying to last through another winter. Sam and Boris spend a part of each day out in the garage, testing the car to make sure it's in working order. The plan is to drive away from here as soon as the weather turns warm. Even Victoria says she is willing to go, but I'm not sure if she really means it. We'll find out when the time comes, I suppose. From the way the sky has been acting for the past seventy-two hours, I don't think we have much longer to wait.

We did our best to take care of the bodies, to clean up the damage, to wipe away the blood. More than that, I don't want to say anything. By the time we had finished, it was the following afternoon. Sam and I went upstairs to take a nap, but I wasn't able to sleep. Sam dropped off almost at once. Not wanting to disturb him, I climbed out of bed and sat down on the floor in a corner of the room. My old bag happened to be lying there, and for no particular reason I started to look through it. That was when I rediscovered the blue notebook I had bought for Isabel. The first several pages were covered with her messages, the short notes she had written to me during the last days of her illness. Most of the messages were quite simple—things like "thank you" or "water" or "my darling Anna"—but when I saw that frail, overlarge handwriting on the page and remembered how hard she had struggled to make the words clear, those simple messages no longer seemed very simple at all. A thousand things came rushing back to me at once. Without even stopping to think about it, I quietly tore those pages from the notebook, folded them into a neat square, and put them back into the bag. Then, taking one of the pencils I had bought from Mr. Gambino so long ago, I propped up the notebook against my knees and started writing this letter.

I have kept at it ever since, adding a few more pages every day, trying to get it all down for you. I sometimes wonder how much I have left out, how much has been lost to me and will never be found again, but those are questions that cannot be answered. Time is running short now, and I mustn't waste any more words than I have to. In the beginning, I didn't think it would take very long—a few days to give you the essentials, and that would be it. Now the entire notebook has almost been filled, and I have barely even skimmed the surface. That explains why my handwriting has become smaller and smaller as I've progressed. I've been trying to fit everything in, trying to get to the end before it's too late, but I see now how badly I've deceived myself. Words do not allow such things. The closer you come to the end, the more there is to say. The end is only imaginary, a destination you invent to keep yourself going, but a point comes when you realize you will never get there. You might have to stop, but that is only because you have run out of time. You stop, but that does not mean you have come to the end.

The words get smaller and smaller, so small that perhaps they are not even legible anymore. It makes me think of Ferdinand and his boats, his lilliputian fleet of sailing ships and schooners. God knows why I persist. I don't believe there is any way this letter can reach you. It's like calling out into the blankness, like screaming into a vast and terrible blankness. Then, when I permit myself a moment of optimism, I shudder to think what will happen if it does wind up in your hands. You'll be stunned by the things I have written, you'll worry yourself sick, and then you'll make the same stupid mistake I did. Please don't, I beg of you. I know you well enough to know you would do it. If you still have any love for me at all, please don't get sucked into that trap. I couldn't stand the thought of having to worry about you, of thinking you might be wandering around these streets. It's enough that one of us has been lost. The important thing is that you stay where you are, that you continue to be there for me in my mind. I am here, and you are there. That is the only consolation I have, and you mustn't do anything to destroy it.

On the other hand, even if this notebook finally gets to you, there is nothing that says you have to read it. You are under no obligation to me, and I would not want to think I had forced you to do anything against your will. Sometimes, I even find myself hoping that it will turn out that way—that you simply won't have the courage to begin. I understand the contradiction, but that is how I sometimes feel. If that is the case, then the words I am writing to you now are already invisible to you. Your eyes will never see them, your brain will never be burdened by the tiniest fraction of what I have said. So much the better, perhaps. Still, I don't think I'd want you to destroy this letter or throw it away. If you choose not to read it, perhaps you should pass it on to my parents instead. I'm sure they would like to have the notebook, even if they can't bring themselves to read it either. They could put it somewhere in my room at home. I think I would like that, knowing it had wound up in that room. Up on one of the shelves above my bed, for example, along with my old dolls and the ballerina costume I had when I was seven—one last thing to remember me by.

I don't go out much anymore. Only when my turn comes to do the shopping, but even then Sam usually volunteers to take my place. I have lost the habit of the streets now, and excursions have become a great strain on me. It's a question of balance, I think. My headaches have been bad again this winter, and whenever I have to walk more than

184

fifty or a hundred yards, I feel myself beginning to wobble. Each time I take a step, I think I'm going to fall down. Being indoors is not as hard on me. I continue to do most of the cooking, but after preparing meals for twenty or thirty people at a time, cooking for four is almost nothing. We don't eat much in any case. Enough to stifle the pangs, but hardly more than that. We're trying to hoard our money for the trip and mustn't depart from this regime. The winter has been relatively cold, almost as cold as the Terrible Winter, but without the incessant snows and high winds. We've kept ourselves warm by dismantling portions of the house and throwing the pieces into the furnace. Victoria was the one who suggested it, but I can't tell if this means she is looking ahead to the future or has simply stopped caring. We've taken apart the banisters, the door frames, the partitions. There was a kind of anarchic pleasure to it at first—chopping up the house for fuel—but now it has become merely grim. Most of the rooms have been stripped bare, and it feels as though we are living in an abandoned bus depot, an old wreck of a building slated for demolition.

For the past two weeks, Sam has gone out nearly every day to comb the perimeters of the city, investigating the situation along the ramparts, watching carefully to see if troops are massing or not. Such knowledge could make all the difference when the time comes. As of this moment, the Fiddler's Rampart seems to be our logical choice. It is the westernmost barrier, and it leads directly to a road that takes you into open country. The Millennial Gate to the south has also tempted us, however. There is more traffic on the other side, we have been told, but the Gate itself is not as strictly guarded. The only option we have definitely eliminated so far is the north. There is apparently great danger and turmoil in that part of the country, and for some time now people have been talking of an invasion, of foreign armies gathering in the forests and preparing to strike the city when the snow melts. We have heard these rumors before, of course, and it is difficult to know what to believe. Boris Stepanovich has already obtained our travel permits by bribing an official, but he still spends several hours every day lurking around the municipal buildings in the center of the city, hoping to glean some scrap of information that might be useful to us. We are lucky to have the travel permits, but that does not necessarily mean they will work. They could be forged, in which case we stand to be arrested the moment we present them to the Exit Supervisor. Or he could confiscate them for no reason at all and tell us to turn back. Such things have been known to happen, and we must be prepared for every contingency. Boris therefore continues to snoop and listen, but the talk he hears is too muddled and discordant to be of any concrete value. He thinks this means that the government will soon be out of power again. If so, we might be able to take advantage of the temporary confusion, but nothing at this point is really clear. Nothing is clear, and we continue to wait. In the meantime, the car sits in the garage, loaded with our suitcases and nine jerry cans of supplementary fuel.

Boris moved in with us about a month ago. He is a good deal thinner than he used to be, and every now and then I can detect a certain haggard look in his face, as though he were suffering from some illness. He never complains, however, and therefore it is impossible to know what the trouble is. Physically, there is no question that he has lost some of his bounce, but I don't think his spirits have been affected by it, at least not in any obvious way. His principal obsession these days is trying to figure out what we will do with ourselves once we leave the city. He comes up with a new plan almost every morning, each one more absurd than the last. The most recent one tops them all, but I think he secretly has his heart set on it. He wants the four of us to create a magic show. We can tour the countryside in our car, he says, giving performances in exchange for food and lodging. He will be the magician, of course, dressed in a black tuxedo and a high silk hat. Sam will be the barker, and Victoria will be the business manager. I will be the assistant—the luscious young woman prancing around in a skimpy, sequined outfit. I will hand the maestro his instruments during the act, and for the grande finale I will climb into a wooden box and get sawed in half. A long, delirious pause will follow, and then, at the precise moment when all hope has been lost, I will emerge from the box with my limbs intact, gesturing triumphantly, blowing kisses to the crowd with a bright, artificial smile on my face.

Considering what we have to look forward to, it is pleasant to dream of these absurdities. The thaw seems imminent now, and there is even a chance that we will leave tomorrow morning. That was how we left it before going to bed: if the sky looks promising, we will be off without another word. It is deep into the night now, and the wind is blowing through the cracks in the house. Everyone else is asleep, and I am sitting downstairs in the kitchen, trying to imagine what is ahead of me. I cannot imagine it. I cannot even begin to think of what will happen to us out

187

there. Anything is possible, and that is almost the same as nothing, almost the same as being born into a world that has never existed before. Perhaps we will find William after we leave the city, but I try not to hope too much. The only thing I ask for now is the chance to live one more day. This is Anna Blume, your old friend from another world. Once we get to where we are going, I will try to write to you again, I promise.

faber and faber

The New York Trilogy
Paul Auster

The work that made Paul Auster's name, **The New York Trilogy** is the ultimate postmodern thriller – a series of brilliant variations on the classic detective story. Auster stakes out the well-traversed terrain of New York City and makes it over anew as a strange and compelling landscape where identities merge and nothing is what it seems.

City of Glass: Quinn, a writer of detective fiction, becomes enmeshed in a case more puzzling than any he might have written.

Ghosts: Blue has been forced by White to spy on Black. From the window of his rented room, Blue watches Black in his room across the street. But Black is staring out of the window. Who is watching whom?

The Locked Room: When Fanshaw disappears, leaving behind a wife, a baby and an extraordinary cache of novels, plays and poems, his boyhood friend is lured obsessively into the life that Fanshaw left behind.

'A shatteringly clever piece of work . . . Utterly gripping, written with an acid sharpness that leaves an indelible dent in the back of the mind.' *Sunday Telegraph*

faber and faber

A Fine Balance
Rohinton Mistry

Winner of the 1996 Commonwealth Writers Prize
Shortlisted for the 1996 Booker Prize

Set in mid-1970s India, **A Fine Balance** is a subtle and compelling narrative about four unlikely characters who come together in circumstances no one could have foreseen soon after the government declares a 'State of Internal Emergency'. It is a breathtaking achievement: panoramic yet humane, intensely political yet rich with local detail; and above all, compulsively readable.

'This is a work of genius. I cannot begin to review it without saying so. It should be read by everyone who loves books, win every prize, make its author a millionaire. **A Fine Balance** is *the* India novel, the novel readers have been waiting for ever since E. M. Forster and J. G. Farrell.'
Literary Review

faber and faber

The Bell Jar
Sylvia Plath

The Bell Jar is Sylvia Plath's only novel. Renowned for its intensity and outstandingly vivid prose, it broke existing boundaries between fiction and reality and helped to make Plath an enduring feminist icon. It was published under a pseudonym a few weeks before the author's suicide.

'This terse account of an American girl's breakdown and treatment gains its considerable power from an objectivity that is extraordinary considering the nature of the material. Sylvia Plath's attention had the quality of ruthlessness . . . imagery and rhetoric is disciplined by an unwinking intelligence.' Stephen Wall, Observer

faber and faber

Our Fathers
Andrew O'Hagan

Shortlisted for the Booker Prize 1999

Jamie returns to Scotland with his grandfather, the legendary social reformer Hugh Bawn, now living out his last days on the eighteenth floor of a high-rise. The young man is faced with the unquiet story of a country he thought he had left behind and now he listens to the voices of ghosts, and what they say about his own life. It is a story of love and landscape, of nationality and strong drink, of Catholic faith and the end of the old Left. Jamie Bawn's journey home will leave him changed beyond words – beyond the words that darkened his childhood.

'By any standards **Our Fathers** is a powerful novel. As a first novel, it is very remarkable indeed.' *Independent*

'I have scarcely read so silvery beautiful a style when it comes to Scots landscape, nor one so tender when it comes to matters of life and death.' Candia McWilliam, *Financial Times*

'The tang of truth, the irreducible core of humanity lies like a shock in the shuddering heart of this great fiction debut.' *Scotland on Sunday*

'A beautiful, elegiac work . . . required reading for everyone.' Ian Rankin, *Evening Standard*

faber and faber

The Remains of the Day
Kazuo Ishiguro

Winner of the Booker Prize

In the summer of 1956, Stevens, the ageing butler of Darlington Hall, embarks upon a leisurely motoring holiday that will take him deep into the English countryside and into his past . . .

A haunting tale of lost causes and a lost love, **The Remains of the Day** contains Ishiguro's now celebrated evocation of life between the wars in a Great English House – within those walls can be heard ever more distinct echoes of the violent upheavals spreading across Europe.

'A remarkable, strange and moving book.' *Independent*

'**The Remains of the Day** is a triumph . . . This wholly convincing portrait of a human life unweaving before your eyes is inventive and absorbing, by turns funny, absurd, and ultimately very moving.' *Sunday Times*

'**The Remains of the Day** is a dream of a book: a beguiling comedy of manners that evolves almost magically into a profound and heart-rending study of personality, class and culture.' *New York Times Book Review*

faber and faber

Birds of America
Lorrie Moore

Winner of the Irish Times International Fiction Prize 1999

Lorrie Moore's dazzling collection is remarkable for its range, emotional force and dark humour, and for the sheer beauty and power of its language. **Birds of America** unfolds a brilliant series of portraits of the young, the hip, the lost, the unsettled and the unhinged of modern-day America.

'The best American writer of her generation.'
Nick Hornby, *Sunday Times*

'Terse, witty, sprung with jaunty despair – Lorrie Moore is to the short story what Dorothy Parker was to the epigram.'
Harpers and Queen

Please send me

	title	ISBN	Price
_____	The New York Trilogy _Paul Auster_	15223 6	£6.99
_____	Jack Maggs _Peter Carey_	19377 3	£6.99
_____	Oscar and Lucinda _Peter Carey_	15304 6	£7.99
_____	Red Earth and Pouring Rain		
_____	_Vikram Chandra_	17456 6	£7.99
_____	Pig Tales _Marie Darrieussecq_	19372 2	£6.99
_____	Hullabaloo in the Guava Orchard		
_____	_Kiran Desai_	19571 7	£6.99
_____	The Last King of Scotland _Giles Foden_	19564 4	£6.99
_____	Headlong _Michael Frayn_	20147 4	£6.99
_____	Lord of the Flies _William Golding_	19147 9	£6.99
_____	The Remains of the Day _Kazuo Ishiguro_	15491 3	£6.99
_____	The Unconsoled _Kazuo Ishiguro_	17754 9	£7.99
_____	The Poisonwood Bible _Barbara Kingsolver_	20175 X	£7.99
_____	Immortality _Milan Kundera_	14456 X	£7.99
_____	The Unbearable Lightness of Being		
_____	_Milan Kundera_	13539 0	£6.99
_____	The Buddha of Suburbia _Hanif Kureishi_	14274 5	£6.99
_____	Aunt Julia and the Scriptwriter		
_____	_Mario Vargas Llosa_	16777 2	£7.99
_____	Amongst Women _John McGahern_	16160 X	£6.99
_____	A Fine Balance _Rohinton Mistry_	17936 3	£7.99
_____	Birds of America _Lorrie Moore_	19727 2	£6.99
_____	Our Fathers _Andrew O'Hagan_	20106 7	£6.99
_____	The Bell Jar _Sylvia Plath_	08178 9	£6.99

**To order these titles phone Bookpost on 01624 836000
Or complete the order form below:**

I enclose a cheque for £ _____ made payable to Bookpost PLC
Please charge my: o Mastercard   o Visa   o Amex   o Delta
o Switch   Switch Issue No_____

Credit Card No _____ Expiry date _____

Name _____

Address _____

_____ Postcode _____

Signed _____ Date _____

Free postage and packing in the UK.
Overseas customers allow £1 per pbk/ £3 per hbk.
Send to: Bookpost PLC, PO Box 29, Douglas, Isle of Man, IM99 1BQ
fax: 01624 837033 email: bookshop@enterprise.net
http://www.bookpost.co.uk